DOWN THE ISLE

THE ROMANTICS
BOOK TWO

KELLY BRIGHT

Down the Isle is a work of fiction. Any references to historical events, real people, or real places are used fictitiously. Other names, characters, places, and events are products of the author's imagination, and any resemblance to actual events or places or persons, living or dead, is entirely coincidental.

2023 Standards of Starlight Paperback Edition

www.standardsofstarlight.com

ISBN: 978-1-952893-21-6

Cover art by Elizabeth Mackey

CHAPTER 1

CLARA

Okay, I'll admit it.

I'm scared to death of airplanes. But it isn't just airplanes. I'm less than thrilled about ladders, rooftops, elevators that go beyond the second floor, bridges. You know … heights.

I'm terrified of heights. *Terrified.*

If I hadn't been distracted by Sean and his nakedness at the party last night, I never would have climbed out on that hotel balcony.

Wait. I'm getting ahead of myself. Let's focus on the present.

I'm on a big ol' plane right now, strapped into a narrow aisle seat and holding onto the armrests so tightly my knuckles are turning white. They look like they belong to some creepy, thin-skinned creature.

We haven't left the ground yet, but the engines are fired up and flight attendants are showing us life preservers and oxygen masks.

Not helping!

I'm freaking out. Seriously. It's my first time.

A pale, plump lady sitting next to me chuckles every time I twitch. She's knitting. Knitting!

Really, lady?

The young Asian guy on the other side of her and by the window is watching breakdancing videos. He already has the shade pulled down so I can't see out.

Damn him.

It'll be hard to keep from giving one or both of my seat mates a good talking to between here and Miami.

That's where this plane stops. Then I have a three-hour layover before getting on another flight to Grand Cayman. I hear that particular plane is likely to be smaller … and bumpier.

Oh, joy.

I've read the tips, tricks, and things to know. I think I'm as prepared as a first-timer can be.

But so far, everything about the air travel experience is new and scary as hell. Visions of every plane wreck movie I've ever seen are flashing through my head as I look around and try to determine which of my fellow passengers will survive the initial crash and which will succumb to injuries—and sharks—soon after. I don't see many who look like they'll survive long enough to eat the rest of us.

That got dark fast.

I know.

See? I need to get out of this winged death trap. Although they've closed the door and removed the ramp thingy. I don't think they'll let me off.

I sound like a child, even though I'm actually a grown woman. I ought to be over it by now.

Want to hear the funniest part?

I'm a travel agent. And not a travel agent who could quit my job and go work somewhere else. I *own* a travel agency.

I work mostly with wedding clients. I make arrangements for guests traveling to my hometown of Loveland, Tennessee to attend area weddings, or for lovebirds going to destination weddings or on their honeymoon.

It's all great fun. I enjoy my career.

Loveland has become known as a tourist destination with a heavy focus on love and romance. The place is becoming a legend, really. Each year, we get more and more visitors than the last. More and more singles, meeting and falling in love. And more and more weddings. We even have couples returning to try and conceive babies there.

As long as we keep our small town charm, you won't hear me complaining. Tourism is good for business, and business is good.

Our proximity to Nashville probably helps. We're away from the hustle and bustle, but not too far away. And we have plenty of spirit and bustle of our own.

My travel agency is part of a larger wedding services group called The Romantics. It's named after my two best friends and me. We co-own the cooperative. You see, all three of us have fancy, romantic last names.

I'm Clara Darling. Rosalie Flowers owns a flower shop, and Ella Lovelace owns a bridal boutique. Get it?

It would be cringeworthy if it—*we*—weren't so cute. We are cute, if I do say so myself.

We've set up shop in an old factory building downtown that's currently being renovated to look all swanky and posh. We like to think we've had a little something to do with the tourism boom in town. We can hope, anyway.

So why, you ask, would I leave all of that loveliness on land to be hurled through the air and deposited on a Caribbean island? And why would I do it by myself, no less?

I won a free trip.

Lucky me.

One of the resorts in the Cayman Islands that I regularly send honeymooners to did a random draw of their favorite industry professionals and my name came up as the winner. And the travel date? The day after my friend Rosie's engagement party, which had already been planned.

That's right. Today is the morning after I watched one of my best friends canoodle with the love of her life in front of a crowd of onlookers. Let's not forget Penny, the puppy her fiancé got her. Patrick sure wowed everyone with that surprise.

I might die from the syrupy sweetness of it all. That is, if I don't die in a plane crash first.

The knitter sitting next to me leans forward in her seat and asks, "What's got you so worked up? You look like you could use a distraction."

I give her a weak smile and laugh. "You have no idea," I

say. I quickly tell her the basics of my situation—the free trip to the Cayman Islands, Rosie's engagement party, how I'm still feeling a bit jealous over how adorable it all was.

She nods knowingly and listens intently as I talk. When I finish my story, she smiles at me warmly and says, "Well, it sounds like you've had a wild ride so far. But don't worry—things are only going to get better from here."

How does she know that? She doesn't. I appreciate her kindness, though. The distraction is helping ... a little.

"Thank you," I say, but I continue to ruminate.

I almost didn't go on this trip. And even before that, I almost didn't believe that I'd won. A free trip? Who wins such a thing, unless they appear on the *Today Show* or *The Price is Right*? I kept the notification papers in my desk drawer for two solid weeks before I made the phone call to confirm their legitimacy.

Once I determined that the trip was, in fact, a real thing, all inclusive with airfare, I mentioned it to my friends. That was my mistake. Had I thought it through, I wouldn't have made a peep. But I peeped.

Rosalie and Ella immediately insisted I take a chance and go. They said I'd never live it down if I didn't. They even said they'd been thinking about how to get me on a plane soon, so this was a perfect opportunity. *The* perfect opportunity.

I don't know. Rosalie is seeing everything through rose-colored glasses—get it?—now that she's reunited and fallen in love with a guy we went to school with as kids. Patrick Hart has her thinking the world is chock full of butterflies and happiness.

Maybe it is, but my single self isn't quite as enthusiastic just yet.

Life is good, don't get me wrong. But maybe I need a Patrick Hart of my own to open my eyes to the possibilities.

Someday.

I'm not the type to try and force a love connection. It has to happen naturally.

And maybe I'm shy. So, what?

Rosalie and Ella often joke that an eligible bachelor would have to throw himself on the hood of my car to meet me. They're probably right.

Okay, they're definitely right.

Hey, I'm busy. I don't exactly have time for a man in my life. I've got schedules to keep and work to do. I'm at the office late most evenings and often on weekends. It's a necessary part of growing a business.

Or so I tell myself.

A perky blonde flight attendant with cherry-red lips brings my focus back to the present moment. She's walking down the aisle sucking on a piece of hard candy and telling everyone to turn off electronics and place bags below the seats in front of us. She says the captain is preparing for takeoff.

Part of me is glad to be getting on with it. The other part, not so much.

Window Guy turns off his breakdancing videos and places his phone in his pocket. Knitting Lady balls up her work in progress and shoves it into a floppy duffel under her feet.

My pulse quickens as the feeling of impending doom takes a firmer hold on me.

I know!

I need something to distract myself during this flight—for far longer than I could possibly chat with the knitter. Something that will keep my attention so I don't worry about every little bump I feel in the possibly-not-so-friendly skies.

I could call my mom, but I'm not sure I need that kind of negativity right now. Meghan Darling means well, but her relentless criticism doesn't exactly boost my confidence.

Yeah, maybe later, Mom.

As I stare straight ahead, leaning my head back hard against my seat, I steel myself for becoming airborne. A yummy sight catches my eye.

A distraction! Good.

He's a late arrival. He has just stepped onto the aircraft, a jovial smile on his dreamy face and a black guitar case slung over his back. He's wearing jeans and a fitted, long-sleeved black shirt with a ball cap and sunglasses.

He won't be needing that long-sleeved shirt where we're going.

He seems harried, like he just ran through the concourse to keep from missing this flight. Yet, he also seems unbothered by his own tardiness.

He apologizes to a couple of flight attendants at the

front of the plane, ducking his head down to look bashful. They want to be stern, but he instantly wins them over. He has one of those smiles. It's youthful, yet mature in an incredibly sexy way. His reddish-brown hair is a perfect compliment to his olive skin, his strong facial features enhanced by just the right amount of stubble. I can't see his eyes behind the glasses, but I'll bet they are piercing.

Damn. That man ... Wow.

I can almost feel *my* eyes go all lovey like Bugs Bunny's in the old cartoons. There are probably cartoon hearts bursting out in front of my eyeballs right now.

I wanted a distraction. He'll do.

For sure.

Maybe I'll imagine myself talking to Dreamy Guitar Guy.

I have a habit of that. It's sort of a silly game I play. I pick out an attractive man and then imagine a conversation between us. It's less awkward than striking up a real conversation.

I wonder where his seat is ... I'm still lost in my thoughts when I realize he's walking towards me.

He's walking towards me! Oh, oh. Oh!

He stops just short of my row, then pulls his boarding pass out of his coat pocket and glances down at it.

I can smell him from here. Maybe it's my imagination, but I think I smell coconut mixed with something woodsy. It smells delicious.

"Excuse me," he says to Knitting Lady with the same bashful yet endearing smile he used on the flight attendants. "I'm sorry to bother you, but I think you're in my seat. It says it right here on my boarding pass: 24B."

My eyes nearly pop out of my head upon hearing this news. I place a hand over my face while I force my eyelids back down to a normal position.

"Do you mind?" he asks.

Oh, holy shit. He's talking to me now. Me!

I must look dazed. I feel dazed.

"Me?" I reply, my voice higher than usual.

"You," he confirms, smiling like a kid in a candy shop.

I wonder if he always appears this happy, or if he likes what he sees.

Stop it, Clara. That's ridiculous. This man is entirely too much for you. Out of your league. WAY out of your league.

I knew I should have dressed up a little for this flight.

I'm wearing a black leather jacket over a loose, white scoop-neck t-shirt, with black leggings and pale pink lace-up shoes. I guess I look … comfortable. At least, I bothered to put in my gold hoop earrings and tended to my shoulder-length curls. I kept my makeup subtle with a hint of color on my cheeks and a shimmery lip gloss.

"No problem," I say, finally understanding what he's asking.

I stand so Knitting Lady can get up to find her proper assigned seat and Dreamy Guitar Guy can prepare to sit down beside me.

Me! Of all the seats on this airplane.

It's almost enough to keep me from noticing the roar of the engines.

He places his guitar in the overhead bin, his shirt rising above his navel to expose a flat, toned stomach in the process.

Damn. It.

I'm beginning to perspire. I'm not sure if it's nerves about the flight, or the effect Dreamy Guitar Guy is having on me. *Phew.* Something is happening.

I grab the laminated aircraft safety card from the seat pocket in front of mine and use it to fan my face. This might not seem odd, except that I'm still standing in the aisle.

"Warm?" he asks as he slides by me and plops down into his seat.

"Um, yeah," I reply.

"It's only going to get warmer," he says, still smiling.

My, oh my.

I'm here for it.

He looks familiar, yet I can't quite place him. Maybe if he took off his hat and sunglasses.

"Do I know you?" I ask.

He smiles a mischievous grin. "I'm not sure. Do you want to know me?"

And that's how my big adventure begins.

CHAPTER 2

CLARA

16 Hours Earlier, The Evening Before

"Congratulations, you two!" I say cheerfully as I hug Rosie's neck.

She leans into me, the excitement practically bubbling from her pores. Not just oozing … bubbling.

My friend is positively giddy. She looks the part of a happily engaged woman, that's for sure. Pink light from the setting sun dances against her cheeks and exposed shoulders on this warm summer evening.

Patrick is standing behind her, all smiles.

"Oh, Clara," Rosalie says, "thanks from the both of us. You and Ella were so kind to throw this engagement party."

"Ditto that," Patrick says with a grin. "This shindig is rad."

He uses strange words like shindig and rad. Rosie doesn't seem to mind. She says strange words herself, at times, so the rest of us let them be. What else are we supposed to do? We can all see that Rosie and Patrick are a match made in heaven.

"It's nothing," I say with a laugh, deflecting. "Ella and I are delighted to do it. We couldn't let our best gal get engaged without throwing a proper … *shindig* … now, could we?"

They laugh, too, then kiss each other lightly on the lips. There's steam behind the kiss. They're being polite by holding the hot and heavier stuff back.

"Get a room," I say, jokingly.

I wink at my friend, and I feel my face flush when I do.

I'm perpetually bashful when it comes to matters of physical intimacy. It's a character flaw, I suppose. No doubt, it comes from my upbringing. My parents act like sex is a dirty word rather than something we all do for our health and wellbeing.

Rosie reaches out and swats me on the arm. "Yeah, yeah," she says.

We're in the courtyard area of a swanky hotel on the outskirts of Loveland called The Mez. We've set up around the sparkling pool with the intention of taking a dip once the sun goes down. We're in beachy-style party clothes, with swimwear underneath. It's fun! It almost feels like we're on a tropical island somewhere.

Speaking of which, I actually will be on a tropical island, come tomorrow evening. I'm flying out of the Nashville airport first thing tomorrow morning.

Oof.

I'm nervous about flying because it will be my very first time on a plane, believe it or not. I have to consciously push all of the squirm-inducing travel thoughts out of my head.

Focus on the celebration, I tell myself. *Be in this moment.*

I make a clicking noise with my tongue, a reminder to stay present. As I do, I look around at all of the people having fun. The scene is enough to lift anyone's spirits.

"How nice," I mumble. Not sarcastically. I mean, it's actually nice.

The adult swimming party theme was my idea. I'm a travel agent who sends heaps of business to this hotel. It's one of my top recommendations for friends of the brides and grooms who get married around here. The owners quite literally owe me, which is why I decided to host the party here.

"Thank you," Rosie whispers, leaning forward. "You're a good friend, Clara. This party is lovely."

"You'd do the same for me," I say, instantly feeling uncomfortable with the reference to *some* day in the future when I *might* find a man of my own.

Might is the operative word.

We're all aware that I'm looking for love. I don't need to rub it in anyone's face. It's not like Rosie can snap her fingers and make the man of my dreams appear out of thin air.

Can she?

"I *will* do the same for you," she replies. "When it's time, Clarebear, I'll be ready. We'll throw you the most amazing engagement party—second only to this one. I look forward to it!"

I quickly wipe a tear from my eye. Rosie and Ella

have called me Clarebear since we were tiny grade school kids with pigtails and ruffly dresses. They don't do it very often anymore, which makes it all the more special when they do.

"You're sweet," I say softly. "I look forward to that, too. More than you know."

I don't know why I'm crying. I'm not sad. Not exactly.

Things are going to be different now. I'm happy for my friend, but I'm not sure I like what her engagement means for me.

Suck it up, Clara Darling, I tell myself. *Be happy for your friend.*

I will. I am. I promise, I am.

It's just that I might be a wee bit jealous.

I don't want to be jealous. Especially because Rosie went through some unpleasantness before she arrived at the falling in love part. Patrick used to be mean to her when they were kids. The way I see it, their happiness now, as adults, is hard earned.

We've been friends for so long that I was right there in middle school, watching the taunting happen.

If you'd have told me then that Rosie and Patrick would end up engaged, I never would have believed you. Not in a million years. Yet here we are, at their engagement party. They're both good people. I mean, Rosie has always been a good person. Patrick is ... a good person, now.

They deserve all the happiness in the world.

My feelings of jealousy aren't about Rosie and Patrick. I know that. They're about me. I want to find a love of my own someday. The sooner, the better. Although, I'm not sure I'd admit that to anyone. Not even my two best friends, who happen to also be my business partners. We see each other all the time at our wedding services group known as The Romantics. There isn't much we don't share with each other.

Ella arrives to join our group, right on cue. She has a tall, dark, and handsome man on her arm. He's well dressed in a smart polo shirt and linen shorts that cling in all the right places. I don't think we've met him before. Judging by their body language, I'm not sure Ella has met him before tonight, either. That wouldn't be out of character for her. I chuckle.

"There are my girls!" she shouts from across the courtyard. "Come give Mama a hug."

She's taken to calling herself Mama lately. I can only laugh. She's a character, if there ever was one.

"Well, hey, there," I say.

I'm tempted to say more—to ask about the new guy —but I don't.

Ella gives me a sly smile. Her man-of-the-moment smiles, too. I get the feeling he enjoys being paraded around like a show pony.

"Hey," he says, simply.

"Hey," we parrot.

Ella's blonde hair is pulled into a fancy braid and she's wearing dramatic eyeshadow that makes her look like a movie star. She's somehow more elegant than the rest of us—even in swimwear. She drops her hunk-o-man's arm then slides into position beside me and wraps an arm around my waist. She artfully balances a fruity cocktail in the other hand. Like a movie star.

"We're so, so happy for you, Rosie!" Ella says in her deep, powerful voice. She's speaking louder than usual to be heard over the music. The DJ just cranked up Bob Marley. "Isn't that right, Clara?"

Ella pinches my cheeks like an Italian grandmother as she talks, forcing me to smile. She actually is Italian, so I suppose what I'm experiencing is a glimpse into her future. I'm sure she'll pinch her granddaughter's cheeks the same way.

She doesn't introduce us to her … *companion*.

I nod and take a deep breath, attempting to let my jealousy go. This is fun. We're having fun, aren't we?

"Yes!" I say with enthusiasm.

I want to be happy for my friend, I really do. My emotion is genuine. Why do I feel like I'm trying to convince myself, though?

Real talk: I want a love like Rosie and Patrick's. The kind that makes you feel like you're the only two people in the world. The problem? I'm shy and—I'll admit it— uptight. Like, an annoying goody two shoes who can't seem to loosen up. That combination tends to make it hard to find a man.

The way my love life is going, you'd think I spray myself down with man repellant each morning.

"Yeah?" Ella asks, leaning closer to me. "What's going on in that pretty little head of yours?"

I try to keep my smile natural and not let any negativity show. Ella can always tell when there's something wrong with me, so I try to deflect her attention.

"Of course, we're *all* thrilled for Rosie and Patrick," I say, managing to pull off a half-hearted smile.

"Are you sure?" Ella asks, looking at me with a concerned expression. "All of us?"

"Um hmm," I say with a nod as a waiter hands me a glass of champagne.

I thank him and take a sip, hoping it will give me a moment to compose myself. Ella has latched on like a dog with a bone, though, and I can tell she doesn't intend to let the subject drop. Not easily, anyway. I'll have to be firm to throw her off the scent.

"Clara," Ella says, pulling back then putting her hand on my arm. A large gold ring on her index finger catches the light from the sun and sparkles mightily. It looks chic next to her perfectly manicured pink nails. "You know we're always here for you, right? If you ever need to talk about anything—"

"I know," I say, cutting her off before she can finish. My voice is as strong as I can muster. My tone is serious. "Thanks, Ella. I appreciate it. I'm good."

"Of course we're here for you, Clara," Rosie says, echoing our friend's concern. "Are you okay?"

Please, drop it. Leave it be. Leave me be.

"I'm fine," I say. "I promise. I shake my head, trying to brush off the negative thoughts. My gold hoop earring clanks against my bangle bracelets as I raise a hand and tuck a few strands of hair behind my ears. "Just tired from party planning."

We're conversing as if Ella's new man isn't even here. It's weird, but Rosie and I have been through this with her before. It's old hat by now. We'll consider him disposable until Ella informs us otherwise.

We look at each other, a slew of thoughts on the tips of our tongues, yet not being said.

"I'm not buying it, Clara," Rosie says after a moment. "You seem distracted. Something is bothering you."

Patrick doesn't speak, but he looks sympathetic. I get that they care. I *appreciate* that they care.

They can't fix this for me.

"I'm not buying it, either," Ella says, folding one arm across her body.

A hint of teal fabric peeks through the neckline of her dress, and now we know which swimsuit she's wearing. It's fabulous. Heads will turn when she strips down to reveal the curve-hugging design. It's exactly what you'd expect from a woman who owns a bridal boutique.

"You could choose to leave me alone," I say. "You know, it's a thought. Let me be?"

"No way," Ella replies. "That's not how this works. Don't make me say it."

"Say what?" I ask, but I already know the answer.

Rosie's giggling, covering her mouth with one delicate hand. Her nails are a deep red. Her engagement ring stuns, catching light with every subtle movement she makes.

"Don't make me say that you need to get laid," Ella quips. "That's the advice I gave Rosie when she was too uptight, and look! A steady meal of man meat has done wonders for her."

We all laugh.

"Man meat?" Patrick asks with a smile. "Is that what I'm reduced to?"

He doesn't seem embarrassed, though. I suppose I'm embarrassed enough for the both of us. Heat rushes to my face.

"Hush, Ella," I say. "This is a classy party. Rosie's dad and both of Patrick's parents will be here. Not to mention, some of those in attendance are clients or colleagues."

Ella practically growls as she kicks her head back and lets out a raucous laugh. "What the fuck ever," she says. "It's just us here right now, and yeah, I'm making the proclamation. You, Clara Darling, need to get laid. Stat. Find some worthy man meat and sandwich it in between your bliss bread until it's thoroughly saturated with joy jelly. Then shake and repeat."

Her companion raises his brows, appearing to be in full support of this plan.

"Ella!" I say. "Watch your mouth."

I'm attempting to be stern with her, but I'm laughing. I can't help it. I get such a kick out of her spunk and her proclivity for coming up with random alternate names for sensitive pieces of anatomy. She used to focus primarily on female anatomy, but I notice she's branching out to include man meat now as well.

"I'll do no such thing," she says. "It's a clear connection. Cause and effect. Rosie got some man meat, and she's an entirely different gal. The same gal, but also better. Don't you think?"

Rosie shrugs. "She isn't wrong."

Patrick seems pleased with his fiancé's answer. He elbows her playfully, then they nuzzle noses.

I roll my eyes. "If you say so," I reply.

"So, I'll ask again," Ella says. "What's going on with you? Do you need to talk?"

I definitely do *not* want to talk. Not to the whole peanut gallery, anyway.

Not now. Not tonight.

I wrack my brain, trying hard to come up with something that will satisfy my friends and get them off my back. I'm well aware that the tables have been turned in the past.

The day Rosie met—well, technically, reunited with — Patrick's brother, Jesse, at the coffee stand in our building, she was all out of sorts. That was the first day Sonny Hoover and his crew began filming for the documentary being produced about us, too. Ella was the ringleader when it came to picking and prodding at Rosie, but I'll admit, I joined in.

Our banter is part of our trio's charm. I'm not feeling up to being the center of attention this evening, though. I want to stay under the radar while I contemplate things.

So, umm ...

"I'm nervous about flying in the morning," I blurt. "That's all."

I scan their faces for reactions.

Luckily, that excuse seems to do the trick. Ella shifts her weight back onto her heels, and I can tell she's giving me a pass.

Phew!

The conversation moves on. Before I know it, we're talking about planes and airports. I'll gladly talk about travel anxiety all day long if it keeps me from having to discuss my sex life—or lack thereof.

"Take something for motion sickness," Patrick says, helpfully. His impossibly thick dark hair moves gently as he talks.

Leave it to a guy like Patrick to be focused on logistics. He's an architect who thinks in concrete terms. He isn't wrong, though. I'm sure he's been on tons of plane rides. I'm the only person I know who hasn't.

"I probably should," I reply. "Good idea."

I make a mental note to stop by a drugstore on the way home.

"Yeah, and be sure to carry a neck pillow on the plane," Patrick adds, "and a bottle of water. Oh! Take portable chargers for your phone and laptop. You can't count on finding a charging station at the airport that isn't already occupied. People swarm around those things like they're pumping out the very nectar of life itself."

"I guess they *are* the very nectar of life itself, in this digital age we live in, when you get right down to it," I say.

Patrick nods. "You have a layover in Miami on your way to Grand Cayman, right?" he asks.

"Okay, yes," I say, "I do. Miami International Airport, or MIA for short, as us travel industry pros call it. I'll do as you suggest. Thank you. But enough about me. We're here to celebrate the two of you. Will you excuse me? I have some things to check on before the meal is served."

Ella smiles without saying another word about me and my bedroom activities, letting us all know she's ready to move on.

I'm not lying, for what it's worth. A local catering company is cooking fancy burgers with all the fixins. I need to track them down and make sure they have everything they need. Ella took the lead on music and decorations. I'm in charge of the food and beverages.

I'll admit, though, it's also an excuse to get some quiet time. Both things are true.

"Yeah, you go ahead," Rosie says. "Do your hostess duties. You're a fabulous hostess, my dear."

"Are you buttering me up for some reason?" I ask with a smile.

Rosie shakes her head, then shoves me off, playfully.

"Going!" I say.

Ella slaps my butt, then gives me a knowing look before turning her full attention back to Rosie, Patrick, and her man candy. "If you need anything, just let me know," she says over her shoulder, even though she's no longer looking at me.

"Will do. You betcha."

I walk away confidently, but find myself turning to watch my friends from a distance. They're laughing and joking around. I can't help but feel a pang of envy. I'm happy for Rosie, but seeing her so in love with Patrick only highlights the fact that I haven't found my own love yet. Even Ella's silent, nameless man is more than I have on my arm at the present moment.

I appreciate my friends. But I want more.

Poor, lonesome me.

CHAPTER 3

CLARA

It's not like I haven't tried finding love. I've had my fair share of dates, but they've never amounted to anything. I've never felt competent in the dating world.

Maybe that's why I became a travel agent who works primarily with wedding clientele. Maybe I'm living vicariously through them. My job makes it easy to stay busy, and well, it keeps my mind focused on the fairy-tale instead of the nuts and bolts of actually finding and falling in love with a real human being.

I'm afraid it's going to be a long evening. I hope something fun—or funny—happens to cheer me up.

Right on time, I bump into Sonny and three cameramen from his crew. I practically walk right into them as they enter the courtyard with cameras slung over their shoulders. They'll be filming tonight.

"Hey, guys," I say, my voice drawing the words out. "What's up?"

A part of me is beginning to relax and get excited.

About the party, and the trip. Even the filming. Maybe the champagne is helping.

"Hey, Clara," Sonny says with his fatherly, wise smile. "How's the party going so far?"

"So far, so good," I say cheerfully. "The happy couple is right over there." I point in Rosie and Patrick's direction.

Sonny always tells us to pretend the cameras aren't there. I have no clue when we'll see any of the footage. Probably not until the series is done and broadcast on television. That's weird, but it's also fine, at the same time. I'm used to it by now. I'm sure the series will be a boon for business.

One of the cameramen is an attractive redheaded guy I've had my eye on. They've been filming us for weeks now, but Big Red and I haven't had a chance to sit down for a proper conversation. He's right behind Sonny, and our eyes meet.

There's magic there. A spark, anyway. My ... um, lady bits ... make that much clear. A wave of pressure builds between my legs. I cross them, hoping my *situation* isn't obvious.

"Careful," Red says with a smile. "Wouldn't want you to hurt yourself."

"What?" I ask, unsure what he's talking about.

He laughs. "You came tearing through here. Almost knocked old Sonny off his feet."

Sonny shakes his head and rolls his eyes as he laughs, too. "Do you guys have to keep calling me old?" he asks.

"Oh," I say, distracted but intrigued. "Right. Sorry, Sonny. You aren't old, my friend. You're young as a spring chicken. Don't listen to anyone who tells you any different."

He puts a hand on his belly and laughs heartily. "Now, that's what I like to hear. Can you follow me around and say that every hour? Because I think it would help with my self image."

"At your service," I say, and I do a little curtsy. "Look for me in exactly one hour's time."

We laugh together, loosening everyone up.

Maybe this party will turn out to be more fun than I expected. I'm shy, alright, but I wouldn't mind a bit of friendly chit chat with Big Red to make the evening more interesting.

I give Sonny and his crew a friendly wave as they head off in one direction, and I turn towards the kitchen to find the caterers. Hopefully, I'll bump into Big Red again before the night is over. I don't know his name, but finding out sounds like a great place to start.

"See ya," I say.

The music is thumping, and Ella has done an amazing job of decorating the space. There are bright string lights everywhere, casting a warm glow over the tables and chairs set up for our guests. It looks like a fairyland, almost too pretty to be real.

When I arrive at the dining area, Thelma, the head caterer and owner of Spice is Nice, is hoisting large silver platters onto the tops of each table. Her brown skin glistens with perspiration. The platters look heavy, and Thelma isn't exactly a young woman. I dare not ask, but I'd guess she's pushing sixty.

"Hey, Thelma, can I help?" I ask as I approach.

She smiles, then scoffs. "Hey, Miss Clara. You most certainly can not. You aren't on my staff, young lady."

"I don't mind," I say, taking a whiff of the most scrumptious smell of meat and savory sides. "Wait, do I smell brisket?"

She smiles even bigger now, her plump lips stretching from ear to ear. "You do. It's my specialty. I thought Miss Rosie and Mr. Patrick and their guests might like to give it a try, so I added it in. My treat. No extra charge."

Thelma's reputation around these parts is legendary. I've only sampled her food, but if tonight's menu selections taste as good as they smell, we're all in for a treat.

I thank her and give her a quick hug. It looks like she has things well under control, so I decide to keep moving.

I take a slow stroll around the grounds, admiring everything from afar before getting a closer look at some of the decorations. Ella has hung paper lanterns from the trees that line the edges of the courtyard, giving it an otherworldly feel. She's also hung up colorful streamers along with little handwritten signs pointing out various points in our evening's itinerary—including a dessert bar. I make sure to stop by each station as I peruse. We did a good job, if I do say so myself.

Even though this party is for Rosie and Patrick, I'm beginning to feel like something good could happen for me as well. Wouldn't that be amazing?

Don't get too excited, I tell myself. *Stay focused.*

Additional guests begin to arrive and I'm filled with

a new burst of energy. Everyone's eyes are wide with anticipation as they take in the magnificent decor.

Over the hustle and bustle of the crowd, I hear what sounds like a puppy whimpering. That catches my attention.

"What in the world?" I ask, searching through the sea of faces to figure out where the sound is coming from.

The whimpering gets louder, rising until becoming the sweetest little woof. Now, I'm certain it's a puppy. A live one, right here at the party.

"Is that a puppy?" I ask.

The crowd has quieted down as everyone watches to see what's happening. It takes a moment for the DJ to get the memo, but finally, he lowers the volume of the music.

More woofs sound and echo throughout the space. The woofs are adorable, in the way that only a sweet little puppy can be.

I'm pretty sure a puppy would melt every last heart in attendance. Although, I'm not sure how thrilled the hotel owners would be. This place is pet friendly, but according to the official policy, that only includes adult dogs under forty pounds that are house trained and well behaved.

"Sorry!" a man's voice calls out.

I feel responsible for whatever it is that's happening, so I walk toward the man. As I get closer, I realize that I know him. It's Patrick's best friend, Brandon Dobson, and he's holding the cutest little spotted puppy I've ever seen.

I met Brandon a few weeks ago at a dinner party.

He's been spending a lot of time around here and hanging out with the group. Later this summer, he's moving to Loveland from Atlanta. He's a good guy. He makes a nice addition to our circle of friends.

"Aww, how cute!" I exclaim, meeting Brandon and reaching out to pet the pup. "Who is this sweet thing?"

Oohs and ahhs surround us as guests admire the baby dog as well.

"This is Patrick and Rosalie's girl," Brandon says with a proud smile as he adjusts the festive pink bow fastened loosely around the dog's neck. "Only Rosalie doesn't know it yet. I'm here with a very special delivery, on behalf of my friend."

The pup yawns and its wrinkly little lips curl around its stout muzzle. Brandon repositions the sweet girl in the crook of one elbow, and she settles in happily.

"Don't let me stop you," I say as I wave Brandon in the direction of the newly engaged couple. "This is a surprise that Rosie will definitely want to see."

"I'm glad," Brandon says. "I'd hate to be the bearer of anything but a good, wanted surprise."

I smile. "She's been dreaming of a spotted puppy for as long as I can remember. You're the bearer of a brilliant surprise, indeed."

He nods, then follows my gesture toward our friends. When Patrick notices, he whispers something in Rosie's ear, then rushes to Brandon to take the pup into his own arms. Holding the baby where Rosie can't get a good look, Patrick walks backward toward her with a huge, beaming grin on his face.

Most of us in the crowd have already seen the pup.

We gather around, eagerly awaiting Rosie's reaction and what promises to be a feel-good, happy scene.

"Rosie, my sweet," Patrick begins, "I have a surprise for you."

She cranes her neck to see what he's hiding, but she can't. Not yet. "What do you have?" she asks, her face alight with anticipation.

"It's something you said you wanted. You're going to love it. I promise. Any guesses?"

"I don't know, but guessing sounds like fun." Rosie chuckles, and I can't help but notice how the crowd hangs on her every utterance. We're spellbound.

I glance around and see many familiar faces. Rachael Drye, Rosie's friend and flower shop assistant, has moved to a prominent spot near the happy couple. She's grinning from ear to ear. Jesse Hart, Patrick's brother, is beside her, and he looks just as pleased. Hope Gallagher, the young woman who works the coffee stand in our building, stands nearby as well. She rises onto her toes to get a better view.

"Okay, then, my love," Patrick says, his body still contorted to keep the pup out of Rosie's sight. "Take your best guess."

"Hmm," she says, raising a finger to her chin. "Just one guess?"

"That's right," Patrick says coyly. "Just one guess."

The pup whimpers, then lets out a sweet woof. Rosie practically squeals, and the ever-growing crowd cheers them on.

At this point, every new guest that arrives makes a beeline for the delightful scene that's unfolding. Principal Livingston and her husband appear. So do Mike Taylor, the owner of another flower shop in town, and his wife, Barb. A few of Patrick's colleagues from Hart Design+Build arrive as well, including his good buddy, Dean Shay.

"Okay, okay," Rosie says, jumping up and down, she's so excited. "I guess … a puppy! It has to be a puppy."

Patrick glances over his shoulder and smiles at his love. "You think so, do you?"

"Yes!" Rosie exclaims.

"Okay, then, how about I show you?"

Rosie nods enthusiastically. I'm not sure I've ever seen her happier. I know Rosie, and I know what this puppy will mean to her. Sure, she's a dog lover and so the pup is great on its own. More importantly, though, the pup will make Rosie and Patrick feel like a family. It's their first new addition to the family. To *their* family.

Aww. How wonderful.

Patrick spins, carefully moving the puppy into Rosie's view.

As expected, Rosie is awestruck. Her eyes widen and her mouth drops open in surprise. "Oh, oh," she says through happy tears. "Is this little one … ours?"

Patrick nods, happy tears welling up in his eyes, too. "That's right. She's our girl. Brandon has been puppy sitting and brought her here for us. After the party, we're taking her home."

"Home," she echoes. "I like the sound of that."

Rosie quickly darts around Patrick's body to take the puppy from him. "Aww, hi, girl," she says as she cradles it in her arms. The pup seems content snuggled against

Rosie's chest, settling into its new mama with a happy sigh.

"Now, that's something special," Ella says with a smile as she looks on.

"It sure is," I say.

Brandon reaches over and pats Patrick on the shoulder. We're all so very happy for them.

Rosie can't stop smiling. Her face is alight with joy as she gazes at the wriggling bundle in her arms. She looks up at Patrick with an expression that says more than words ever could. Gratefulness, love, and admiration for his thoughtfulness are all blended together in one beautiful moment of happiness.

Tears well up in their eyes as they embrace each other tightly while we—their closest friends—cheer them on.

"What's her name?" Jesse asks.

Patrick nods, then looks at Rosie. "I thought we could call her Penny, since the markings above her eyes look like tiny copper pennies. Pennies have always been lucky for me. It's a thing that goes back to happy memories of my early childhood. Before my parents split up. Before I became an angry kid who teased you at school."

"Hush about that," Rosie says. "That's ancient history. You're different now. We're different."

He nods again. "Right. So the thing with pennies goes way back, to good times. Like the times I know we'll share together. Not just you and me, but our fur babies—Tabatha, Maverick, and now Penny."

Rosie agrees. "The name is perfect. She's our lucky Penny."

They kiss again, as little Penny gazes up at them. She seems to be enjoying the love between her new parents. She woofs, apparently approving of her name.

Penny, it is.

The puppy has stolen everyone's heart. The party atmosphere buzzes with smiles and laughter as we all bask in the glow of this joyous new beginning.

CHAPTER 4

CLARA

"*D*inner time!" Thelma announces. "Come and get it."

Good. I'm starving.

I think I got so wrapped up in packing and party logistics that I actually forgot to eat lunch today. My stomach feels like it has been gnawing at my backbone for hours now.

I help usher everyone to their seats.

"You're going to love this," I say as I sit down beside Ella and her boy toy and get comfortable. Rachael sits on the other side of me.

"You know it," Ella says, never one to miss out on a good meal.

Thelma proudly presents her famous brisket, which is piled on platters and served with all kinds of sides. The smoky aroma from the juicy meat fills the air, eliciting eager compliments from our hungry guests. When we dive in and take the first bites, guests rave about the flavor of the tender dish and can't get enough of it.

"I think we've died and gone to heaven," Rachael says as she dabs the corners of her mouth with a cloth napkin.

"Deliciousness," Ella's man mumbles as his eyes roll back in his head. "Mmmm … savory."

I think it's the first time I've heard him speak. Ella and I look at each other, then break out into laughter. Leave it to Thelma's brisket to elicit words from the man candy. She has a secret weapon.

"I wonder if there's a Mr. Thelma, and if she used brisket to snag him," I whisper to Ella.

"With this brisket, she could probably get him to do her bidding. Anything she wanted!" she replies with a grin. "It's working on Javier."

"Oh?" I ask. "He has a name? And you know it?"

She elbows me. "Of course, I know his name," she replies, then pauses for dramatic effect. "I heard him tell the gatekeeper you hired to man the front door of this place. How do you think we got in? I have to admit, he really gets the lady lube flowing, if you catch my drift. Just look at him."

My eyes grow wide, even though I'm not actually surprised. "You stinker, you," I say.

Ella laughs between bites. We're talking while we eat. "What? You aren't going to call me a slut?" she asks.

"Oh, I wouldn't do that."

"You can," she says with a mouth full. "It's accurate. I intend to have my way with him as soon as this party is over. Hell, I might even have my way with him *before* this party is over. I'm sure we can find a secluded spot somewhere."

I shake my head. "I wouldn't say you're … that word you used. You're my friend. I wouldn't dare—"

"What are you two talking about?" Rachael asks, hoping to get in on the conversation.

"Nothing!" Ella and I reply in unison.

"Just that this food is amazing," I add. "Have you ever tasted anything quite as good?"

"Certainly not brisket this good," Rachael replied. "Thelma is something else. Maybe you should recruit her to be part of The Romantics. Wouldn't a catering business make a nice addition to the group?"

Ella takes a sip of her fruity drink to wash the food down, then expresses her agreement. "Not a bad idea, Rach. Way to keep business goals front and center."

"Yeah, good idea," I say. "We'll have to run that by Rosie when I get back in town. We're definitely looking to expand. Especially once the renovations are complete on our building."

Rachael smiles, proud of herself.

I watch quietly as everyone enjoys their meals, thoroughly impressed by Thelma's cooking skills. I'm glad we chose her for our party, as she truly understands how to make a feast for any occasion. Her generous personality shines through in every bite, making us all feel loved and appreciated.

Rachael's exactly right. Thelma would make a great addition to our group.

After dinner is finished and bellies are full, the hotel's setup crew begins moving tables to create room for a dance floor. Suddenly, we hear a man's voice shouting from somewhere in the distance. I can't place the voice immediately, but it seems familiar.

"My darling!" he shouts. "I'm looking for my darling."

My first inclination is to ignore him. I can't tell where his voice is coming from, but I think he's outside the bounds of our party. That means he isn't my problem.

When he shouts again, guests begin to look at me as if they expect me to take care of it, though. I hope this guy doesn't become my problem.

"My darling! Please," he says.

"Don't worry, folks," I say. "I'm sure the hotel staff will handle this. Probably someone who had a little too much to drink." They keep looking at me, unsure, so I add, "Maybe he had a bit too much fun in Downtown Nashville at the honky tonks. Maybe his darling left him for a country music star."

Jesse laughs out loud, and I appreciate his support. "It happens," he says with a smirk.

The man isn't giving up, though. "My darling! My darling."

"What's up with him?" Ella asks, putting a hand on her hip. "Where is his voice coming from?"

Rachael has one hand over her eyes, blocking the lights as she scans the scene. All of a sudden, she spots him. "Up there," she says, pointing.

"Where?" Ella replies.

Rosie and Patrick are on the other side of the room and too focused on their new puppy to pay much attention, but they stop and look. "You see something?"

Patrick asks.

"On the balcony," Rachael says. "One building over, toward the front of the hotel."

I squint my eyes and look in that direction. It takes a moment, but sure enough, I see him. The man appears to be stark naked. His legs are crossed and he's using one hand to cover his—um, man parts—while he waves furiously with the other. He's tall and his skin is pale, but that's about all I can tell about him from here.

"My darling!" he shouts again. "Up here! I'm locked out."

Tension in the crowd eases as people begin to smile. The thought of being locked on a balcony—*naked*—is funny. I don't care who you are. Sonny and one of his camera guys point cameras in the man's direction. A whirring noise lets us know they're zooming in.

"My darling!" the man shouts again.

"He's relentless, isn't he?" Rachael asks.

"I guess I might be, too, if I were in his position," I reply. "But why does he keep calling for his darling?"

The man turns and tries the door, pulling against the handle dramatically to illustrate that it's locked. "See?" he asks. "I'm stuck out here. I don't have my card key. I need my darling to help!"

His turn means we are all now treated to a view of his backside. Laughter breaks out as the crowd seems to decide that this is all in good fun. I laugh, too. I can't help it. Sure, the guy is actually locked out. *Probably*. But he seems good natured about it. He isn't mad that we're laughing. We're laughing with him, not at him.

"Wait," Sonny says while peering through the lens of his camera. "That's Sean."

"Our Sean?" the other camera guy asks. "The redhead, Sean O'Shea?"

"As in the redheaded cameraman?" I echo.

"The one and only," Sonny says.

The poor guy. I wonder how he got himself in that predicament. And who in the world is his darling? I didn't know he had a girlfriend. Then it hits me, like a ton of bricks. The realization dawns on Ella at the same time.

"He isn't saying my darling …" I muse.

"He's calling for you, *Clara* Darling," Ella says, finishing my sentence.

Sonny's camera pans my way to capture my reaction. I am mortified. Color rushes to my cheeks.

Oh.My.Gosh.

"Um, I—" I stammer. "I don't know what's happening here."

"Clara Darling!" Sean calls. "Help me out. Please! You're the party planner, right? I lost my card key. It's a long story. A little help, please?"

Ella chuckles. "That's one way to get a man undressed, Clara. Points for creativity."

"Stop it," I reply with a laugh.

I'm so embarrassed that he was calling my name. I *barely* know the guy. I certainly didn't realize he knew my full name. By the looks of things, people might assume otherwise.

But it's funny. I'll admit, it's very, very funny.

I guess I should be the one to rescue him. "Be back in a few," I say to my friends.

I take a deep breath and steel myself for the task at hand. I pull out my phone and call hotel security. They are surprisingly helpful. Within minutes, they arrive in the lobby and walk with me to let Sean back in.

As we make our way up the elevator, I can't help but be amused by the situation. It sounds like Sean got himself locked out of his room by leaving his card key inside. He was probably in such a rush to get back down to the party that he didn't even think twice about it. As to the question of why he went out on the balcony instead of to a phone to call the front desk, I have no idea.

I wanted something funny to happen tonight. I'd say this fits the bill. Our guest won't soon forget this spectacle.

When we reach the balcony, Sean is still standing in exactly the same spot with his hands clenched tightly to his body, trying to keep himself warm against the evening breeze. The crowd is still there too—some of them laughing, some of them snapping pictures on their phones as if this were part of a staged show rather than a real-life event.

"Clara Darling!" Sean exclaims when he sees me. "You're just in time."

He reaches out to shake my hand excitedly before remembering that he's in a, well, *compromising* position.

I can't help but notice his washboard abs and muscular physique. I keep my eyes up and on his face as much as possible, but I let them wander for a split second.

Let's just say the view is amazIng.

Um, um, umm.

"Oops," he says. "I guess this can't get any worse. So, there's that."

"Go get dressed," I reply. "You can tell me the story later."

"Is that a promise?" he asks.

I shrug playfully. "Sure. I wouldn't dare miss the salacious details that left you out here like this."

"Then it's a date," he replies.

Everyone down below claps as he waves and bows before disappearing back into the hotel.

Once we're sure that Sean is tucked safely back indoors, I return to the party. Everyone peppers me with questions about how he ended up locked on the balcony. I laugh and shake my head, trying to get the words out of my mouth between giggles. I honestly say that I don't know, but hope to find out sometime soon.

It isn't long until I hear a familiar voice coming from behind me. It's Sean. He has one of his camera crew buddies with him, and they're talking about the party as if nothing out of the ordinary has happened.

"Nice, huh?" Sean asks his friend.

"Oh, yeah, for sure," the other guy replies. "But I'll bet we could crank things up a notch."

Sean laughs a hearty belly laugh. "Shouldn't we wait until their dinner has settled? It's still early."

He's a big guy, at over six feet tall. I'm 5'8" and he has at least a few inches on me. I could wear heels and he'd still be taller than me. He looks like a real-life viking, now that I think about it. The clothes he changed into are nicer than the grungy t-shirt I saw him in earlier. He looks ready for the party now, complete with a cowboy hat.

How Nashville? Or should I say, how Loveland?.

Appraising him this way—and seeing him on the balcony *that* way—is making me all tingly.

I blush. *Uh-oh*.

"What's wrong, Sean?" his friend asks. "You too old for a good party? Maybe we should tell Sonny that you'll take over the role of the token old man on the crew."

"*Sean*," I say out loud. "I really like that name."

What I don't say out loud is that I like the way our names sound together—Sean and Clara. That has at least as nice a ring to it as Patrick and Rosie, right?

It's silly. I know.

I know.

I catch their attention and Sean lifts his head to look at me, but his friend pulls him away just as our eyes meet. I turn my back, feeling like I probably shouldn't have been eavesdropping.

Is that what I was doing? I think I've seen way too much this evening.

Suddenly, the DJ's music stops and everyone turns to watch as Big Red—*Sean*— takes the microphone. He grabs an acoustic guitar and swings it up and around his neck as if he's made the motion a thousand times. He grins and looks out over the crowd before speaking.

"Let's get this party started," he says with a laugh and a smile.

The crowd cheers in agreement, then Sean motions for a live band to take the stage. Instantly, the area is filled with soulful sounds of lively music that gets everyone into rhythm and grooving on their feet. Drinks flow freely as people start enjoying poolside cocktails such as margaritas, pina coladas, mojitos, and sangria. Guests are dancing in pairs or alone as they sway to the beat of the music, smiles stretching across their faces as they surrender to its contagious energy.

The atmosphere is electric.

I had no idea Sean was a musician. He sings, too, and he's good.

As the night wears on, the party gets even more lively. I get even more relaxed.

The music gets louder and Rosie and Patrick are the center of attention, but I'm content to stay on the sidelines and watch them enjoy their moment. I catch glimpses of Ella's elegant frame as she moves around the pool, making sure everyone is having a good time. She's always been a force to be reckoned with, and I admire her for it.

I breathe a sigh of relief as the current song comes to an end. This party is going well. Even better than I expected. My job here is almost done. Ella and I pulled it off. It's been an evening that Rosie and Patrick will always remember.

Thank heavens, I think.

Out of nowhere, Sean turns his microphone towards

me, making my heart skip a beat. "How about joining me up here for a song?" he asks with a smile.

What in the hell? What's this guy doing?

"Who? Me?" I ask.

"That's right. You, Clara," he says.

Well, we've established that he knows my name.

I blush—big time—and shake my head. "I don't know the words."

I don't say that I can't sing. I actually can sing. I spent six years in honor choir as a kid, then I minored in vocal performance in college. I'm a mezzo soprano. But how did Sean know any of that? Was it a lucky guess?

He laughs, "Don't worry, I'll teach you the words. Come on up here and let's have some fun."

His eyes twinkle with excitement as he extends his hand to me.

I can hardly believe I'm doing this, but I take it and let him lead me onto the stage. We stand side by side. He holds his guitar while I hold the microphone in front of us both. He begins strumming the strings, playing a soft melody that rises into a crescendo as the band joins in with their instruments.

It doesn't take long for me to recognize the song. It's the old romantic classic, "It Had to Be You." I remember my parents singing along to this when I was a kid and they watched *When Harry Met Sally*. The song—and the movie—reminds me of a time when my parents were happy and in love.

I know all of the words.

The crowd cheers for us as we start singing together, our voices blending harmoniously.

I find myself swaying to the music, following Sean's lead as he steps from side to side. He catches me off guard by putting his arm around my waist and spinning me in a circle, eliciting more cheers from the crowd.

It isn't long before everyone is singing and dancing along with us, clapping their hands and tapping their feet in time.

As the song ends, Sean takes my hand and we bow together, smiling wide as everyone applauds our performance. We make our way down the stage steps and join the other dancers on the floor.

I can feel the energy of the crowd as they cheer and clap for us. I can see it in their eyes, in the smiles on their faces. They're excited, happy to be here celebrating this special moment. It's Rosie and Patrick's party, but somehow, it's become a special night for me, too.

I'm not sure how it happened. I'm not sure who to thank.

I look up at Sean and he smiles back at me, giving my hand a gentle squeeze. I'm filled with warmth and gratitude for his willingness to share.

The sky turns a cool dark blue, signaling that the day has ended. On Ella's cue, everyone rushes to the pool, excited for an evening swim.

We've got colorful floats with ring tosses, beach balls, and a few pool noodles for when we want to play Marco Polo. The lights of the pool turn a brilliant blue as we all climb in and start to swim around together.

Couples cling to each other as they dive in, and children splash about in their own joyous way. Even Rosie and Patrick take a few daring dives into the water together, holding hands as they dive out of sight before resurfacing again with a laugh.

After a while, it turns into one big splash-splash session with people bombarding each other with water balloons and squirting their friends with water guns.

The sun sets behind us and soon enough it's dark outside. No one minds because we are all lit up from within by love and friendship. We set our floating lanterns off into the night sky like glowing stars above us. The light reflects off of the pool creating beautiful patterns everywhere we look.

The night is full of joyous energy as people frolic around in the pool, making memories that will last a lifetime. Even I'm caught up in all of it despite my initial feelings of jealousy—I can't help but join in.

It's a good night.

I have miles to travel in the morning and I don't know what fate has in store, but tonight is a very, very good night.

CHAPTER 5

SEAN

The Next Morning

I've had my eye on Clara since day one of filming at The Romantics building. She probably doesn't know that. At least, I hope not. I've tried to play it cool over the past couple of months. I've tried to take it easy.

Clara is the shy one in her group of friends. The one who wouldn't make the first move, if she liked a guy. The one who watches her best friend get engaged and would never admit that she wants to be next. The one who is wound so tight, I'll bet she has no idea what she's missing in life. The one who needs a good man like me to broaden her horizons.

That's why I'm taking her on a romantic getaway. Sort of.

"Make a left here," I say to Sonny. "North on I-65."

He's driving me to the Nashville airport. It's a thirty minute trip from Loveland when there's no traffic. This morning, though, we didn't leave early enough to beat the crowds. The interstate is mobbed, chock full of people out and about, even though it's Saturday.

"Got it," Sonny says. He looks at me quizzically, then asks, "You do realize I've been to the airport before, right? And also that I have GPS cued up?"

I sigh. "Yeah, that sounds about right. I guess I'm nervous."

"Loosen up," he urges.

"Okay," I reply. "Take your time. My plane doesn't leave for several hours. Ignore my mansplaining."

Sonny laughs. "Does it count as mansplaining if you're a man explaining to another man?"

"Who knows?" I ask. "Forgive me, anyway."

My mind is elsewhere.

You see, Clara won an all-inclusive trip to Grand Cayman Island in the Caribbean, courtesy of a resort where she sends a lot of travelers. The way I understand it, the resort wants to reward travel agents like Clara for referrals while also giving them an up close and personal look at the place. I'm sure they figure she'll sell even more travers on choosing their property if she's seen it in person. A win-win.

So, where do I fit in? Good question.

When I overheard Clara talking about the trip and that she'd be traveling all alone, I decided to find a way to Grand Cayman for a chance to get to know her.

My plan came together easier than I'd originally thought. Sonny wanted one of us camera guys to get some footage of Clara at the resort. I jumped at the chance and volunteered before any of the others could.

But that wasn't the end. I wanted to have my own thing going on in Grand Cayman as well, so I didn't appear clingy. I wouldn't want to follow her around the whole time, like a weirdo. So, I booked a gig playing guitar.

When I'm not filming Clara or hanging out with her, I'll rehearse for and play the gig. I'm hoping to make it big in the country music world someday, and every single gig gets me one step closer. This could be a solid opportunity for me.

The way I see it, I'm killing two birds with one stone. Another win-win, right? What could go wrong?

My intentions are pure. *I promise.* I want Clara to experience the world in a way that she hasn't before.

"What do you have planned?" Sonny asks, bringing my attention back to the present. "For Clara. How are you going to woo her?"

"How do you know I want to woo her?" I ask.

Sonny lowers his nose and gives me a look that says it all. He wasn't born yesterday. "Really?" he asks. "I've seen the way you look at her. Not to mention, that naked man stunt on the balcony last night. You wanted an excuse to give her a front row seat to the gun show."

I pause, but only for a minute. "Okay, you've got me there. I do plan to woo her," I say. "But that is not a crime. I'm more than willing to be a fool … for love."

He laughs. "Okay, Romeo, run your plan by me. Maybe I can help," he offers. "I've learned a thing or two about women in my—ah hem—certain number of years on this planet."

Is Sonny even married? He doesn't wear a wedding ring. I don't think I've heard mention of a wife. Oh, well. Married or not, he can probably teach a young lad like me a few things.

I lean forward in my seat. "Okay, I'll lay it all out for you."

He nods. "Go."

"Once we get checked in and unpacked, I figure we'll start off with a drive through some of the most beautiful countryside she's ever seen," I explain. "The sparkling blue sea and lush green forests will make it seem like an enchanted paradise. When we stop for lunch, I'll choose a restaurant overlooking the water. I'll enjoy watching Clara's face light up as she gazes at the stunning view."

"And then?" Sonny asks.

"Then, we'll spend more time exploring the area together with its white sand beaches, crystal clear waters, and vibrant foliage. We'll watch the sunset from a special spot on top of a limestone hill known as the Bluff. I hear it will provide us with a great view of the landscape below."

"Then?"

"Then," I continue, "we'll head back to the resort. If pictures online are any indication, the place is amazing."

"Yeah?"

I nod. "It's an exotic beach resort known for its luxurious spa treatments, relaxing atmosphere, and panoramic views. My hope is that Clara will be transformed into another person—one who is more open and relaxed than ever before."

"Sounds like a decent plan," Sonny says. He eyes me

carefully. I'm not done yet, and he knows it. "I get the sense you have more in store?"

"Righto," I say with a laugh. "I was planning on booking a romantic dinner at the resort. My hope is that it will be an experience that neither of us will forget. I've even planned the menu—fresh seafood and international flavors, served by candlelight in an intimate beach setting. We can enjoy the night while listening to live music from local artists. After the meal, we can take a stroll along the white sand beach or go for a moonlit swim in their pool. Somewhere during our trip I plan on renting jet skis so we can explore more of Grand Cayman together."

"You've really thought this through," Sonny says.

"I have," I reply. "I've had plenty of time while on assignment in Loveland. I don't know anyone in the area. Or maybe I should say I didn't know anyone. I know you clowns now."

Sonny laughs and gives me a friendly bump on the arm. "Clowns, huh?'

"What would you call us?"

"Okay, so, you consider yourself a clown, too?" he asks.

"Of course," I joke. "I might be quiet until you get to know me, but I can clown with the best. Been doing it since Mrs. Miller's class in second grade."

Sonny laughs again, but then his mood turns serious. "Just be careful. Okay?"

I look at him, confused. "Careful ... with what, specifically?"

"With Clara. With love. Not to mention, with your

professional role in filming footage for our docu-series," he explains. "The last thing I want is trouble. Don't let me hear that you've been harassing one of our clients."

I wrinkle my nose. "I can't believe you went there," I say. "I'd never risk your professional reputation, Sonny. Or mine."

"Just be careful. Please."

I nod and look away, feeling like I'm not quite ready to explain my interest in Clara any further. We have a good working relationship, but I feel like there is something more beneath the surface waiting to be explored. To me, this romantic vacation could be the perfect opportunity to get to know her better—to find out what makes her tick and if there is a chance for something real between us.

It has been difficult for me to open up and connect with people in the past, but ever since meeting Clara, I can't help but feel drawn to her. There is an air of mystery about her that captures my attention, and a playfulness behind her eyes that intrigues me. She's witty and intelligent, with an artist's eye for detail. I want to learn more about her.

"You can tell me what's on your mind," Sonny says. "I didn't mean to make you clam up. We have, at least, fifteen more minutes before we arrive at the airport. Twenty, if I take Briley Parkway."

I grab a bottle of water from my bag and take a sip, then I look at Sonny, trying to decide whether I should explain further why I'm interested in Clara.

"The truth is, there's something special about her," I begin. "She has this calm and confident demeanor that draws me in. We connected right away when we met and I can't help but think that this trip could be the start of something special for us. After spending time together exploring the area, relaxing at the resort, and enjoying dinner together under the stars, who knows what might happen? Plus, you have to admit that it would make for great footage!"

"Except that you're the cameraman. Who will do the filming?" he asks with a laugh.

"That's merely a detail to be worked out," I say, smiling. "I can also position the camera somewhere stationary and let it record. I'll edit later."

He lowers his brow and appraises me. It kind of feels like I'm back in high school, waiting on a verdict from my guidance counselor after telling her I only wanted to go to college so I could play basketball. I thought she might choke me right there and then when I dropped that bombshell.

"Sean, are you sure about all of this?" Sonny asks. "You've only known Clara a short time, and as far as I can tell, you've barely spoken to her."

I hesitate. He's right. I don't want to rush in, if that isn't the right thing to do. I don't want to get so caught up in the drama and enchantment of this trip that I overdo it and scare her off. After a moment to collect my thoughts, I speak.

"If it doesn't work out, then no worries. At least, I will have taken my shot," I say. "We need the footage, anyway. Right?"

Sonny gives me another long look, then nods in agreement.

"I suppose you're right," he says. "Just make sure you get some great shots while you're there and that they are edited properly when you come back. If you need any help with the editing process, let me know. I'll be more than happy to lend a hand."

"Thanks, man," I reply. "I will."

He doesn't know about the gig. I could tell him. I'm sure he'd be supportive. I decide not to, though. I don't want Sonny to question my dedication to the docu-series. Besides, making it big in the country music world is such a long shot. I mean, it's why I took on this filming project in Loveland in the first place, since it's such close proximity to Nashville, but I know better than to get too excited about my musical ambitions. If a career in country music happens, it happens, but being a cameraman is real life, for the time being. It pays the bills and keeps me busy. There's no shame in that.

"You know what, Sonny?" I ask, my tone serious.

"What's that?"

"You remind me of my Uncle Finn. You look so much like him, I swear, you could be mistaken for siblings. You're a good dude like him, too."

Sonny smiles. "That sounds like a compliment."

"It absolutely is," I reply.

He looks at me hard, realizing there's more that I'm not saying. "Where is this Uncle Finn now?"

I chuckle. "Sanibel Island, Florida," I say. "By way of Boston, and originally from Cork, Ireland. Finn and my dad emigrated to the States when they were young kids. They've always been close, which allowed me to be close to my uncle, too. He's sort of a second father to me. And one of the best men I've ever known. I don't know what I'd do without him."

"I thought you might be Irish," Sonny muses.

"What?" I tease, "did the name Sean O'Shea and the ginger hair give it away?"

Sonny nods. "Maybe."

We ride in silence the rest of the way to the airport. As we do, I think about my Uncle Finn and how this trip could change my life—for better or for worse—and I can't help but feel excited about the possibilities ahead of me. I think about the adventures Clara and I could have and how amazing it would be to capture it all on film.

My heart races at the thought of being able to watch our journey together in HD after we have returned home. Well, after the series airs, but you know what I mean.

When we arrive and Sonny pulls up to the curb for departing flights, I get my bags and my guitar out of the back and bid him farewell.

"One way or another," I shout as I step away and toward the terminal, "I'm coming back a changed man!"

"See you next week," he says with a laugh.

"See you next week."

I give him a mock salute, extending a finger to my brow and waving it away. Then I turn and walk into the airport, ready for my grand, romantic adventure.

CHAPTER 6

CLARA

On the Plane

I smile, then sit down clumsily, collecting my thoughts. I need to make some kind of sense of what I'm feeling.

My terror at the imminent takeoff. The handsome stranger sitting beside me. The fact that I swear I know him from somewhere.

It's a lot at once.

For now, I decide to ignore Dreamy Guitar Guy's question about whether I want to know him. I mean, I *do* want to know him. But I'm not sure I should admit it right off the bat. Wouldn't that be … I don't know .. *cringe*? Is that what the young people call it these days?

I take a deep breath and try not to sound uncomfortable.

"Right. You mean that it's warm in Miami, where this plane lands," I confirm, glancing at him as I talk. "I suppose so. Never been there."

"Really?" he asks, buckling his belt then nodding hello to Window Guy on the other side of him.

"Yep," I reply. "It's my first time …" I almost tell him I'm new to air travel, but think better of it. "In Florida."

"Florida is a nice place," he says. "Sparkling water, wide sandy beaches, beautiful people. You'll fit right in."

Is he flirting with me? I think so.

Holy shit.

Also, I think I detect a hint of a Massachusetts accent. So many other dreamy guys are from Massachusetts: John Krasinski, Chris Evans, Matt Damon, Mark and Donnie Whalberg, Ben Affleck, Matt LeBlanc … just to name a few. But that's beside the point.

I laugh, not sure if it seems forced. Hopefully not.

"That's sweet," I say. "Sounds lovely."

He grins. "Oh, it is," he says with a knowing nod. "I've been to Miami a few times. It's an interesting place, full of interesting people and things to do."

We start talking about travel—where we've gone and our favorite places—and I tell him about my plans for a dream trip to Miami: visiting the Everglades National Park to see the alligators, exploring an outdoor art gallery called Wynwood Walls, visiting Little Havana and eating at one of the local Cuban restaurants there, taking a boat tour around Biscayne Bay, surfing or paddle boarding on South Beach … the list goes on.

I've sent plenty of travel clients to Miami. One day, I intend to go and do all the things myself. One day when I have more than just a layover in the city.

He then shares stories from his own trips—going out for drinks in South Beach's chic bars, meeting new friends at late-night clubs in Downtown Miami, relaxing by the pool in Key Biscayne after a long day of sightseeing.

It all sounds fabulous. Truly. *Fabulous.* To a reluctant traveler like me, it sounds like a dream.

He reaches his thick hand sideways to shake mine. My mind wanders as I think about what he might do to me with those hands.

Rosie and Ella assume I'm too straight laced to let my mind wander into the gutter. I might not be as wild as either of them, but my mind goes places. It's going places now.

Uh hum.

"Pleased to meet you," he says.

He still hasn't taken off his hat or sunglasses, which is strange. I'm looking at my own reflection in his aviator frames.

"Clara Darling. Same."

He chuckles. "Well, aren't you just a fairy tale character waiting to happen?"

"How so?" I ask, already knowing the answer.

I get plenty of comments about my name. I know the routine.

"My darling?"

"Never heard that one before," I say, a smile tugging at my lips.

Something about the way he says *my darling* is familiar.

"Oh, yeah," he confirms, pleased with himself. "I love to come up with obvious things and pretend I'm the first."

Window Guy laughs, egging him on.

"You like the attention?" I kid. "I couldn't tell."

He winks at me. Then Window Guy gives him a fist bump. They're getting a kick out of this.

"What are you doing in Miami?" he asks, leaning his head my way.

I quickly debate whether I should tell him. I'm not one for giving details of my life to complete strangers, but something about this guy is disarming. It's hard to keep my guard up around him, even though we just met.

This man might be trouble ... Trouble of the delicious kind.

Why do I keep thinking about the word delicious?

"I'm only there for a layover," I say.

"Really?" he replies. "Where to?"

"Grand Cayman," I say proudly.

I'm suddenly more excited about the trip. I feel like a real traveler now. I'm leaving the United States. I'm an *international* traveler. I might call myself worldly, even. As long as no one reminds me we're still on the ground in Nashville. That pesky takeoff process will surely dampen my mood.

Speaking of that, I wonder what's the holdup.

"Ha!" he says, inexplicably.

"What makes you say that?" I ask. "Ha! What?"

He places a big, warm hand on top of mine. A jolt moves through me.

"I'm going to Grand Cayman, too," he explains. "What are the odds?"

I stare into his eyes—err, sunglasses—too mesmerized to speak. He keeps his hand in place. It feels good. Like … It's a perfect fit on top of mine. For a moment, it feels like we're the only two people on the plane. Bugs Bunny eyes and all. I feel like a Cinderella who just put on her slipper.

It fits! It fits!

Yet, it feels familiar. What the what? Have I touched him before?

"I … Wow …" I manage. "Of all the places. Right?"

Window Guy chuckles. I don't even care. Until the moment is rudely interrupted by takeoff.

The flight attendants are gathering at the front of the plane as the Captain comes on the speaker system to confirm. "Flight attendants, prepare for takeoff," he says in an official voice. They strap into jump seats, smiling as if this is no big deal.

It's a big deal. Holy hell.

I take my hand away from Dreamy Guitar Guy so I can go back to gripping the armrests. He smiles curiously, then laces his fingers together on his lap. He looks straight ahead, but I can feel him eyeing me with his peripheral vision—from behind the glasses.

I'm embarrassed to be so scared of flying, but I can't help it.

The engines on the airplane suddenly rev into overdrive. At least, that's what it sounds like. The whir is louder and more powerful. Meanwhile, an even higher pitched zingy noise begins. It seems to have something to do with the flaps on the wings. I can see movement on the wing through one of the tiny round windows across the aisle. Window Guy still has his shade closed on our side.

Oh, my God. Are they testing the mechanical parts on the wings? They are! This can't be good. Why now? Why ...?"

My mind races as I think about the sheer number of moving parts on an aircraft and how every single one needs to be maintained and in working order if we want the plane to stay in the air. I run through a list of dreadful possibilities in my mind ranging from the airplane being a lemon to the pilots being drunk. None of them make sense. I know that. But I'm frightened anyway.

The plane jerks as it begins to move. My stomach does a flip inside me, and not in a good way.

"I think I'm going to be sick," I mumble as the plane taxis to the runway.

I only know we're taxying because I read about it. I also read that takeoff will involve such force that I'll be pushed back into my seat. And I don't want to go through that kind of an experience. I want out of this plane. Right now. Dreamy Guitar Guy or not. I can't do this.

I can't ...

"Take a few deep breaths," he says quietly, whispering to my ear so no one else hears. "Come on, in for four counts then out for four. I'll do it with you. 1-2-3-4 ..."

I close my eyes, trying to remember what the flight attendants said about barf bags. I read about those, too. Although I'm not sure this plane has any.

Do they have them? Where ...?

I force back the sickness rising in my throat.

"Relax," Dreamy Guitar Guy says. "Listen to the sound of my voice. In - 2 - 3 - 4, and out - 2 - 3 - 4. It's okay, Clara. You can grab onto my hand or arm if you want to. Looks like you're giving those armrests quite a squeeze."

As he says my name, I begin to calm down. It sounds right in his mouth.

The plane makes a turn and then stops. I know what it means. It's time for the fast part, and there's no escape. We're going into the sky, whether I like it or not.

I decide to take this guy up on his offer. Greedily, I lace one arm through his, gripping it tightly. Then I lean my head down on his bicep, which he flexes. Maybe the flex is on purpose, or maybe not. I keep my eyes closed, oblivious to everything around me except the airplane and the alluring man I'm holding onto.

I know I probably look ridiculous. I know Window Guy is probably laughing his ass off. He might even be videoing me by now. I honestly don't care.

Suddenly, the plane lurches forward and I feel the force push me back. My heart beats so loud I think it might thud right out of my chest. My stomach twists and turns. But my guy leans his cheek gently on the top of my head.

"It's okay," he reassures again. "This is all perfectly normal. Nothing to be concerned about. Hold onto me. I'll keep you safe."

It's an intimate moment. One I never expected. Not in a million years. I wonder what Rosie and Ella would say if they could see me now.

The engines roar as we race down the runway full speed ahead. It feels like I'm a kid on a scary amusement park ride with no power to make it stop. I am totally vulnerable. I don't like it. Maybe because being a vulnerable kid didn't go so well for me back in the day. I've worked hard to claw my way to an independent adulthood. And this plane ride is reminding me just how precarious any real control over my life is.

Damn it.

"Thanks," I say, my head still burrowed into the side of his arm.

"No thanks necessary," he says sweetly.

I get a whiff of the coconut again. I wonder if it's in his deodorant. Or his body wash, maybe? Perhaps he chose the scent in preparation for travel to the tropics. Whatever it is, I want more. I inhale.

"Deep breaths," I mutter, since it seems like I should explain myself.

Surely, he already thinks I'm weird. Sniffing him probably doesn't help.

In a flash, behind my tightly closed eyes, I see a vision of him on the beach. A light breeze makes palm trees sway in the distance as the sun sparkles on bright blue water. He's holding two drinks in coconut shells and hoisting one in my direction. Tropical flowers encircle blue straws. They're eye-catching, but not nearly as much as the sight of him in swimming trunks, his muscles glistening with some sort of body butter.

"Yes," I say under my breath, unable to help myself.

The scene looks amazing. *He* looks amazing. It looks like something right out of a dream. My dream. And to think, I haven't even been to the tropics before. I'll bet it's all better in person.

I can hardly wait. Especially if he and I bump into each other on Grand Cayman. Perhaps I should spend some effort making sure that happens.

All at once, I feel the lift. We're in the air.

We're in the air!

"See, you did it," he says softly, my grip on his arm still strong.

That wasn't so bad. Thanks to him.

He smiles, then turns his head toward me and slowly —finally!—takes off his hat and sunglasses. I gasp, genuinely shocked by the sight before me. No wonder he feels so right.

"You!" I say.

He shrugs. "Me … and you."

"Sean O'Shea, you clever devil. I knew you were familiar, but your hat and sunglasses made for a good disguise."

"So, now I know you'll get cozy with any old guy that shows up and says nice things to you on a plane," he jokes. "Noted."

I swat his arm playfully. "It's better because it's you," I say.

He nods, and leans closer.

We both laugh and the plane rumbles beneath us, but I don't feel quite as scared anymore. Instead, I begin to plan activities for our time on Grand Cayman. We talk about what we want to do and see while we're there. I suppose it's the travel agent in me. Planning an itinerary helps me relax.

Snorkeling in the clear blue waters of the Caribbean Sea? Exploring the island by bike? Sightseeing in George Town? Check, check, and … check.

As we discuss all of our options, I realize how lucky we are to have stumbled into one another's lives at just this moment.

I know. That sounds mushy. Cheesy, even. But hear me out. I've had my eye on this delicious man for weeks.

After last night at the party … and now being here together, like this …

It kind of feels like if Sean is by my side, anything is possible. We decide that no matter what we end up doing on Grand Cayman, it will surely be a trip for the books—full of adventure and unforgettable memories made together.

Adventure awaits. *Swoon.*

CHAPTER 7

SEAN

My plan seems like it might actually work. I think Clara digs me.

I'm sitting here, beside her pretty face and shapely body, and she's leaning into me. I can't tell you the thrill I feel knowing that she's comfortable with me. That she's drawn to me, apparently, the same way I'm drawn to her.

So, what if I had to finagle things a bit to make it happen? I couldn't help but want to take her away from the hustle and bustle of the film set in Loveland. I want to show her a world that she's never seen before. A romantic getaway in a faraway place filled with beauty, romance, and adventure.

Doesn't every man want that for the woman he cares about?

I don't know. Maybe I'm more of a grand gestures guy than most. But so, what if I am?

The idea of whisking her away to the Caribbean island filled my heart with joy. For weeks now, I've imagined her eyes lighting up from the very thought of spending a week exploring an exotic paradise. It might never have happened without her winning this trip, but I'm sure glad it did. We're here, now. Together.

I lean back in my seat, flashing a grin at the beautiful woman sitting next to me. She's beginning to calm down, but her anxiety is still evident. "So, Clara, first time on a plane?"

She bites her lip nervously and nods, her eyes flickering to the window. "Yeah, could you tell? I'm a little scared."

I reach over and pat her hand reassuringly. "Don't worry, I'm a seasoned traveler. I'll protect you from any turbulence. Or whatever else. Um …" I'm rambling. "What I mean, is that I'm at your service."

She laughs, a sound that sends shivers down my spine. "Thanks, I feel better already."

"Really?" I ask.

She nods. "Really. I do."

A mischievous smile plays on my lips as I seize this opportunity to tease her a little. After all, it's not like we're complete strangers. Clara and I are familiar with each other. I'm part of the camera crew filming a docu-series on the wedding services group she co-owns with her two best friends. We've exchanged pleasantries and smiles, but we never really had a chance to connect on a deeper level. Until last night at Rosalie's engagement party. And now.

I lean back in my seat, my eyes never leaving Clara's figure. I can't help but notice her slight fidgeting. Her wide eyes dart around the cabin, her body tense with apprehension. The urge to put her at ease overtakes me. I must do something else to help her settle.

"Want to know the real reason I'm here?" I whisper.

It's a gamble to tell her the truth so early, but I feel like she has a right to know. I'd want to know, if the roles were reversed.

"You mean, the reason you're on this plane?" she asks. "I'm guessing that's because you're on your way to Grand Cayman, right? Is there something I missed?"

I smile. "Just thought I'd come to keep an eye on you. Wouldn't want the turbulence to get too friendly, would we?"

"Wait," she continues, "Did you ask Sonny for the assignment? So you could film me?"

I nod. "Well, not film you … like *that*, exactly. Unless you want me to."

A faint blush tinges Clara's cheeks, and I know I've hit the right note. My playful nature often has that effect on people, but with Clara, it feels different. There's a spark there, an undeniable chemistry that I can't ignore.

"I'm not mad," she says simply.

"Good thing, because I'm already here," I reply with a grin.

As the plane hits a bit of turbulence, Clara grips the armrest tighter, her knuckles turning white. I reach out and gently place my hand on top of hers, intertwining our fingers. "Hey," I say softly, "You're doing great. Trust me, flying's a breeze. Pun intended."

A smile tugs at the corners of her lips, and her grip on my hand tightens ever so slightly. It's a small gesture, but it's enough to fill me with a warmth that spreads through my body.

Even though we're on a crowded plane, it feels like we're the only two people here. I'm not sure I've ever felt like this before.

I like it. And I like my chances of spending much more quality time with Clara Darling. My darling.

Soon, the seatbelt sign switches off, and the captain announces that we've reached our cruising altitude. I release Clara's hand and lean back, settling into the seat comfortably. "So, tell me," I begin, breaking the silence, "What's it like to be a jet-setter?"

Clara's nervousness fades as she opens up, sharing her dreams and aspirations. She talks about her love for travel and her desire to create unforgettable experiences for couples getting married. The passion in her voice is infectious, and I can't help but be drawn to her energy.

I nod, genuinely impressed. "You know, I'm a bit of a traveler myself," I say, leaning in closer. "And I don't always capture moments with a camera. Sometimes, I capture them with words and melodies."

Clara raises an eyebrow, curiosity twinkling in her eyes. "You're a songwriter?"

I nod, a hint of pride lacing my voice. "That's right. Been strumming my guitar and scribbling lyrics since I was a teenager. It's my way of making sense of the world."

A thoughtful expression crosses Clara's face. "That's amazing. I've always been fascinated by music, but I can't carry a tune to save my life. Not that I've tried. I like to stay in my own lane."

"Understood," I reply.

After a moment, she asks tentatively, "Could you write a song for me? Like, how long would it take you … if you did?"

I laugh, enjoying the banter between us. "Oh, trust me, Clara. I could write a song for you right here, right now. But fair warning, it might end up being a cheesy tune about love and airplanes."

Clara raises an eyebrow, her eyes sparkling with mischief. "Oh really? I'd love to hear it. Give it your best shot, Mr. Songwriter."

I grin, feigning deep thought as I reach into my pocket for a pen and a small notepad. I start scribbling notes, pretending to be in the midst of creating a masterpiece. After a few seconds, I pause dramatically and look up at Clara. "You know what? I have a better idea."

Her curiosity piqued, Clara leans closer, waiting for me to reveal my plan.

"I want to take my time and write a proper song for you," I say, a mischievous glint in my eyes. "But I think I owe you a little something for challenging me, don't you think?"

Clara grins, nodding eagerly. "Absolutely. What's the plan?"

I pull out my phone and start typing furiously, my fingers dancing across the screen. "Well, Clara, you're about to witness a little something called spontaneous musical eruption."

She laughs, and her eyes widen with curiosity as I explain. "I'm going to send a note to a few people on the plane, and they'll pass it on to others. When the time is right, on my cue, they'll help me out. Trust me, it'll be epic."

Clara's laughter fills the air, and her excitement is palpable. "I can't believe you're doing this. Okay, I'm in. Let's make this plane the stage for your little performance."

With a smirk, I hit the airdrop button on my iPhone, sending the lyrics to "It Had to Be You" along with a message to everyone on the plane who shows up as available to receive it.

The message reads, "Pass the word: On my cue, sing it loud for Clara!"

As we sit there, waiting for the perfect moment, I glance at Clara, her eyes shining with anticipation. She has little idea what's about to happen, and I can't wait to see her reaction.

Finally, I nod to the flight attendant standing nearby, who gives me a subtle thumbs-up. It's time.

I take a deep breath and stand up, raising my voice slightly. "Ladies and gentlemen, if I could have your attention for just a moment. We have a special surprise for someone on this plane. Her name is Clara."

All eyes turn to Clara, who blushes and looks at me in astonishment.

"Are you gonna play your guitar?" the young Asian guy sitting next to the window asks. He's been listening to Clara and I chat, no doubt. And he surely saw me board the plane with the guitar case. I appreciate the dude's enthusiasm.

I look at the flight attendant. "Do you mind?"

She winks and nods. "Go for it."

Once my guitar is in hand, I clear my throat and start to sing, the words flowing effortlessly from my lips. "It had to be you, Clara. It had to be you. I've wandered around, finally found somebody who ... makes me be true."

As I sing, the sound of another voice joins in, and then another. The melody fills the cabin as the passengers around us begin to sing along, their voices blending in a harmonious chorus.

Clara's eyes widen in sheer delight, her smile growing bigger with each passing second. The surprise on her face is priceless, and it fills me with a warmth that radiates through every inch of my being.

The song spreads like wildfire, enveloping the entire plane in a shared moment of joy and celebration. People who were strangers just moments ago now come together, united by music and the desire to make Clara feel special.

I suppose everyone loves a feel-good love story, right?

I watch as Clara's eyes well up with tears, her laughter mingling with the lyrics of the song. The spontaneous musical eruption becomes a testament to the power of connection, the magic of love, and the joy that can be found in unexpected moments. Clara is surrounded by a symphony of voices, each one singing her name, their genuine affection and admiration filling the air.

Overwhelmed by the sheer beauty of the moment, Clara stands up, her face radiant with emotion. She raises her arms, joining the chorus of voices, and the whole plane erupts in applause and cheers.

As the song comes to an end, I make my way back to her, a satisfied grin on my face. The passengers begin to settle down, their voices fading into whispers of awe and delight. Clara looks at me, her eyes shimmering with tears of joy.

"Sean, I ... I don't even know what to say," she stammers, her voice filled with emotion. "You sure do know how to make a girl feel special."

I take her hand, squeezing it gently. "You don't have to say anything, Clara. That moment was for you. I wanted to give you a memory you'd never forget."

Clara wraps her arms around me, pulling me into a tight embrace. "Thank you, Sean."

I hold her close, reveling in the warmth of her embrace. "You deserve every bit of it, Clara. You bring joy to people's lives with your passion for travel and your beautiful spirit. I couldn't resist the chance to make this trip unforgettable for you."

We stay in each other's arms for a moment, basking in the afterglow of the musical spectacle. The air is thick with an unspoken connection, a newfound understanding between us. I realize that this plane ride has sparked something very real, and I don't want it to end.

"Clara," I whisper, my voice laced with sincerity, "I meant what I said earlier about writing a proper song for you. I want to take the time to craft something that truly captures who you are. Would you let me do that?"

Clara pulls back slightly, her eyes meeting mine. Her smile is both playful and hopeful. "Only if you promise to sing it to me one day."

I chuckle, my heart pounding with excitement. "Deal. I'll pour my heart into that song, and one day, I'll sing it just for you."

We settle back into our seats, our fingers intertwined. The plane continues its path, but something has shifted. Our connection has deepened, and as we exchange glances and laughter, I know that this unexpected journey has opened up a world of possibilities for us.

Together, we watch as the clouds dance outside the window, a backdrop to our newfound romance. And as the plane carries us forward, I can't help but feel grateful.

CHAPTER 8

CLARA

By the time we arrive in Miami, I can feel the heat. And I don't just mean from the warm air outside.

There's a smolder between Sean and me that might catch fire any minute now. We're in sync, finishing each other's sentences, leaning on each other, and smiling so big our faces can barely contain our expressions. I've never experienced anything like this.

I'm a shy girl who sits things out. It's not that I have social anxiety or anything like that. I'm comfortable around people. But when it comes to dating— or being the center of attention, really— I prefer to keep my distance. I enjoy more of a supporting role.

My relationship history proves it.

There was Benton Harris, my high school boyfriend who I dated during my senior year. He was a rugby player with dirty blonde hair and a great body that lured me like a moth to a flame. And not the good kind of flame like the one burning between Sean and me right now. Benton deflowered me in unceremonious fashion, then moved on to a more popular and outgoing girl. I was crushed. My dad had to practically shove a Wendy's cheeseburger down my throat on day three of not eating after the breakup. It was intense.

Then there was Roy Harby, my college boyfriend. He was moody and brooding with shoulder-length curly black hair, but he was good to me. That lasted all of a few months my junior year. He was better than Benton. At least Roy and I were actually in love. I think. We sure did make a lot of love in the back of his beaten-up Chevy station wagon. But he, too, moved on to someone more extroverted.

At that point, I began to consider that my shyness was a problem. Guys apparently like risk takers who will do strenuous outdoorsy things with them and go to noisy bars. My idea of a good time is quieter. More low-key. I can't change it anymore than a tiger can change its stripes.

Michael Peterson was the best of the bunch. Ours was the only real adult relationship I've had. We were together for nearly a year, and we talked seriously about getting married. He was handsome with deep brown skin and broad shoulders. We made plenty of love, too. The sex was amazing. I couldn't loosen up enough to go through with a wedding though. I hesitated. Something wasn't right, so I put on the brakes. I decided it was better to wait until I knew for sure.

Shouldn't everyone?

Michael lived near me in Loveland until he moved to San Diego for a promotion. I took his transfer as a chance to end things. Long distance relationships sound hellish, anyway. It was time for us to split. I was devastated, but in a more mature way. I knew it was the only course of action. No one had to shove food down my throat.

I admit, the resulting dry spell might have been avoided if I'd put myself out there more instead of burying myself in work. Rosalie and Ella insist I'm holding myself back.

Maybe I haven't found the right person yet. Maybe when I do, I'll know it right away. Maybe things will be effortless between us. Maybe it will feel like it does right now … with Sean.

Come on, Clara. That's crazy. You two hardly know each other. He's essentially a stranger.

I try to talk myself out of love at first sight as we step off the aircraft and into the Miami International Airport terminal. I don't think I've ever been happier to feel solid ground under my feet. Dare I say flying was sort of fun, but I'm in no hurry to do it again anytime soon. Which means I'll have to hype myself up before the flight to Grand Cayman.

Sean is walking a few feet ahead of me, but he keeps glancing back as if he's making sure I'm still here.

"I'm here," I say, smiling coyly.

We haven't talked about whether we're going to stick together during the three-hour layover. For all I know, Sean was just being friendly on the plane. He might not want to see me now that we're at the airport. I have no real knowledge about his life. Not really. For all I know, he's meeting a significant other.

God, I hope not.

"Good," he says, winking at me.

When we reach the waiting area and the crowd from the plane begins to disburse, Sean plops his guitar down on a seat and then sits himself down beside it. He looks up at me with those come-hither eyes and pats the empty chair on his other side.

"Have a seat," he instructs.

I hesitate, not sure how interested I want to appear. I definitely don't want to seem desperate.

I'm no good at the dating games people play.

"What are we doing?" I ask.

Damn. I shouldn't have said we. Too late now.

"That depends," he replies. "What do you want to do?"

I like how he rolled with it. Maybe there is a we. Or at least, maybe there can be.

"I don't know," I say, glancing down at my smart-watch. "We have just about three hours until the next leg. And I imagine we need to be on the plane at least thirty minutes before takeoff, right?"

"Maybe," Sean says, a smirk on his lips.

"Oh, right," I add, remembering. "You were our late arrival. You barely made the flight."

"It happens," he replies, running a hand through his thick hair. "We have time for some fun."

I smile. I'm not sure I should give in to this beautiful man, but I want to.

"Okay, I'm game. What do you have in mind?"

"Well," he begins, licking his lips. This ought to be good. "You said you've never been to Miami before ..."

"Yeah, so?"

"How about we call a car and do lunch in Miami Beach? I know a great burger place across the street from the beach. We can eat, then swim."

My eyes light up at the thought. I can feel them practically glowing with excitement. But Sean's plan sounds risky.

"How far away is that?" I ask.

"We could be there in twenty-five minutes. Twenty, if traffic is light."

"Wow," I mutter. "I had no idea it was so close."

Sean leans over and rests his head on my shoulder, then looks up at me with the sweetest expression.

"I'd like to take you," he says. "Come to the beach with me."

"I don't have a swimsuit," I add. "It's in my checked bag."

"We can buy you one at a cute little seaside boutique. It will be a souvenir. Part of the adventure."

"Will it now?" I ask, unable to hide the interest on my face. "A seaside boutique does sound kind of special."

"Indeed. I'll buy you something to remember our day together."

Sean blinks his puppy-dog eyes. He looks too good to refuse.

Mercy me.

I'm a grown woman with responsibilities. And travel arrangements. I can't run to the beach on a three-hour layover.

Can I?

There's no time to text Rosalie and Ella to ask what they think.

I quickly run through a list of what-ifs in my head.

What if Sean is a bad guy and he takes me somewhere sketchy? What if he robs me? Or worse, beats me up and leaves me in an abandoned alley somewhere. I talk myself off that ledge as quickly as I hopped on. After all, he's been filming the docu-series at our building for weeks. Surely, Sonny vetted him before adding him to the crew.

Sean seems fine. And besides, I can call the car so it's all in my name. I can foot the bill and be in control of where we go. And if I'm robbed ... I suppose I'd call the police and my credit card companies. Not the end of the world. My wealth is diversified, like experts recommend. No single robbery could clean me out.

I move on to the next question forcing itself to the front of my brain. What if we don't make it back in time for the flight to Grand Cayman? I didn't purchase travel insurance. I probably should have, since I own a travel agency and all. But I didn't. If I miss the flight, I'm out a few hundred bucks. Not to mention, my hotel stay is nonrefundable at this point. I'd be stuck forking out extra for a new flight, and for a hotel room in Miami, depending on timing.

I try to look at the positives. The change costs wouldn't be prohibitive. I can afford to cover the additional expenses if necessary. Hey, maybe I can look at them as the costs associated with having a memorable adventure. People pay more to take their families to Disney World for a day.

Fine.

With all of that settled, I'm left with the most pressing questions.

What if I don't have any fun? And oh, but what if I do? What if I have the time of my life? Will I ever be the same? Will I ever *want* to be?

To hell with it. I'm in.

"Okay," I say, smiling.

"Okay?" Sean asks. "You'll go?"

"Yep. Let's do it. Let's blow this popsicle stand."

Sean jumps out of his seat like an excited kid.

"Yes!" he hisses, exaggerating the "s" sound. "You're going to love it, Darling. Miami Beach. Let's go to South Beach, actually. That's where all the art deco and beautiful people are. You'll see. We'll eat, then shop, then swim. We'll have so much fun!"

We practically run through the concourse, stopping just long enough for me to call for a car. Sean hands me a wad of cash to chip in, making it easy to maintain control over the driver-hiring experience. I might be paranoid, but it puts my mind at ease.

The car is there waiting by the time we step out through the sliding glass doors into the humid South Florida air. Easy peasy.

My heart pounds as I slide into the backseat, Sean slipping in behind me.

"To South Beach," I say to the young, dark-skinned driver. He seems pleasant. He winks at us as we pile in together, probably happy to see a couple in love.

Wait, did I just think...

"On our way," the driver replies.

CHAPTER 9

CLARA

$\mathcal{T}$he ride is fast, like Sean said it would be. Before I know it, we're surrounded by some of the most gorgeous scenery I've ever laid eyes on.

I'm dazzled as I gaze out the window at the brilliant blue waters of the Intracoastal Waterway and Biscayne Bay. I'd seen these waters in photos, but nothing could have prepared me for the real thing. It looks as if someone turned up the brightness and the vibrance on everything outdoors.

What a sight to see! Loveland is pretty in its own right, but it's completely different than the breathtaking sights of Miami.

I can't wait to tell my clients about this. My first-hand experience will serve them well, which makes me think that I should start traveling a lot more. I mean, don't I owe it to my clients to check things out and report back?

It's suddenly a whole new world.

I don't want to speak poorly of Loveland. It's my

hometown, after all. And it has its undeniable charm. But oh, my. Miami is breathtakingly gorgeous. How have I been missing this all of my life? Thank the heavens that I finally got my ass on an airplane so I could see more.

Rosalie and Ella were right. Spot on, in fact. I owe them a huge thank you. I make a mental note to pick up something nice to bring back home to them.

That reminds me ... I should be taking pictures of all of this. I want to remember it. And I need to show my friends. I can hear them squealing and giggling now. It's something we do together. Every bit of good news is reacted to as if we're the guests of honor at a rowdy party.

I pick up my smartphone and begin snapping shots out the window. Sean smiles for a long while, apparently proud to be expanding my horizons. He gives me a chance to take it all in without interrupting. And I do take it *all* in. I roll down my window, breathing the ocean air like a dog on a joyride as I hang my head out. Tall buildings line the streets while palm trees sway. Boats fill marinas and dance in the open water. Fishermen cast lines as they waste the day away.

Once I've settled down, Sean leans across my lap playfully and positions himself in front of my camera. His hands rest wide on my thighs.

"Do you like the view, Darling?" he asks.

I love the way he's calling me Darling. It's my last name. In public, it's a secret that only we know.

I smile as my, um, lady parts tingle, thanks to Sean's hands being in such close proximity. In a flash, I imagine those hands moving up, up, up ... his thumbs meeting in the middle as his palms and fingers cover my hips.

"I do," I reply in a purr.

He's making me feel all gooey. It's hard to keep my composure.

Sean's face is inches away from mine. He looks at my lips, which I've just parted absentmindedly. He's thinking what I'm thinking. Or, what my body is thinking. I'm not sure my brain is in charge anymore.

"That's good," he adds. "Because I sure do like what I see."

I close my eyes as I smile even bigger, breathing his coconut-tinged scent in. I half expect him to kiss me. His lips would feel amazing on mine.

I know they would.

But he doesn't kiss me. Not yet.

Instead, he returns to his side of the backseat, giving my midsection a tickle as he goes. His touch is electric. And he wants to touch me more. I can tell.

"I'm taking pictures for my friends," I mumble, hoping I sound at least somewhat coherent. "They'll want to see this."

"Ah, the Romantics," he replies. "Ella and Rosalie."

"That's right," I reply. "Good memory."

"Well, I *have* been on the crew filming all three of you for the docu-series," he teases. "But I must admit, I've only had eyes for *you*. Since the day I walked into The Romantics building. I pay attention when something is important. Or should I say, when someone is important?"

I smile.

"Hey, get a picture of me to show them," Sean offers. "They'll be surprised that we're together here."

I do just that, holding my phone in the air as he sports a dashing grin.

"Got it," I confirm with a laugh.

"Now one of us together," he prompts, leaning his cheek flush against mine.

I hoist the phone up, switch it to selfie mode, and snap.

"Another," Sean says, turning his face around and placing his lips on my cheek.

I snap.

"One more," he says, lifting a hand and turning my face toward his, our lips finally meeting in a kiss. He puts his other hand on my side, just above my hip. This time, it's a firm, sexy grip instead of a tickle.

I snap the photo.

OMG! OMG!

It's like fireworks are going off inside my body. Fireworks!

His lips are positively delicious, just like I thought they'd be. I'm in ecstasy. I'm one-hundred percent certain that I've never felt this alive.

He chews gently on my bottom lip as he licks the edges, then our tongues meet and slowly explore each other. After a sensual moment, Sean presses his entire mouth against mine, then gingerly pulls back.

"Send the ladies that one," he suggests with a huge grin.

Our driver chuckles, apparently enjoying this.

"Okay," I manage, my face feeling flush.

"And would you look at that?" Seans says assuredly as he glances down at the photo on my screen.

"What?" I ask.

"Now we have a picture of our first kiss." He leans over and gives me a lingering peck on the lips. "The first of many … I hope," he mouths.

Shut the front door.

I am officially putty in this man's hands. My body is on fire for him. I want him. Right now.

What have I even been doing with my life?

Whatever this is, I want more. I'd leave everything for it. I'd follow him anywhere.

Anywhere. I need more.

Maybe Rosalie is right. Maybe the world is chock full of butterflies and happiness. Screw my workaholic tendencies and busy schedules.

Before I know it, the driver has the car in park and is urging us out. "Enjoy this beautiful day, lovebirds," he calls as we collect ourselves and step onto the South Beach sidewalk.

Sean grabs his guitar from the trunk and slings it over one shoulder. Somehow, he still manages to hold the door for me and help me with my bag.

Can I just say? I'm so smitten right now. I'm walking on air. It feels like I'm in the best dream I've ever had, and I never want to wake up.

Mmm, mmm, mmm.

The sun seems like it's set to max brightness, making everything it shines on sparkle in the most alluring way. Across the road is the beach. It's smooth and sandy right up until it meets the sea, which is a soft blue color. The waves lap gently on the shore.

I feel like I've been transported to an entirely different world. Maybe I have. I got on that plane and was hurled into the sky. For all I know, this isn't even Earth anymore. Maybe we went all the way into space and to somewhere different. This doesn't feel like any Earth I've experienced. It's a multitude of times better.

As I look around at the crowd, I immediately realize Sean was right. The people are beautiful. Few are fully clothed, and no one seems to mind. Scantily clad men and women are enjoying themselves. Some are on rollerblades or bicycles. Others are strolling along, seemingly without a care in the world. Many are holding hands.

"See," Sean says as he laces my fingers into his and gestures with a tip of his head. "I told you that you'd fit right in."

I nod, too overwhelmed for words. Although, I feel inappropriately dressed. Sean seems to know what I'm thinking.

"How about we change plans? Shop first, then eat?" he suggests.

"Yes," I reply. "Find me something pretty."

I want to look good for what promises to be a memorable day.

"This way," Sean says. "There's a swim shop down about a block from here. They should have what you need. If I remember right, they have dresses and other clothing, too."

"Perfect," I say, leaning my head back and feeling the sun on my face.

A rush of excitement fills my body as I hear Sean mention dresses. I'm a girly girl. I like dresses, especially summertime frilly ones. I take good care of myself and know I'm physically attractive. I want to show him how good I can look.

Sean leads the way, pulling me carefully behind him as we weave in and out of the crowds. I'm not sure where it comes from, but Better Together by Jack Johnson reaches our ears. It isn't Jack himself, but rather someone else playing a cover of his song live. The music seems to be coming from one of the restaurants. Sean and I bob along to the beat while we walk towards the sound.

Everything feels timeless here. It doesn't matter that Better Together was released years ago. It's a happy song with a beachy vibe. It fits. Like my imaginary Cinderella slipper.

As we reach the front of the restaurant the music is coming from, I see couples dancing in front of a small stage. They're spilling out onto the sidewalk in front of us, blissfully unaware of anything else.

Sean stops and turns to me.

"Darling, may I have this dance?" he asks as he raises my hand in the air and dips his chin.

"Right here?" I ask. "Now?"

"Why not?" he answers.

I take a breath and let the good vibes wash over me. The amazing setting. The warm air. The music. The happy, dancing people. The drop-dead gorgeous man in front of me.

My real-life dream continues.

"Okay," I reply, grinning. "If you insist."

"Oh, I definitely do," Sean says as he pulls me to him and begins to sway.

Our bodies interlock like they belong together. There's no awkwardness. Only easy togetherness. His arms fall loosely around my waist, and his hands meet in the small of my back. My arms find their way around his neck and rest comfortably behind his head. We gaze into each other's eyes as we move with the music.

I feel safe with Sean. I can't explain why, but it feels like we've known each other for ages. He feels familiar. We're surrounded by hundreds of people right now, but it feels like it's just the two of us. It doesn't even matter where we are or what's happening around us. I get the distinct sense that it would always be this way … If we spent the rest of our lives together.

Really? So soon?

Doubts attempt to creep in as my head and my heart duke it out. But I don't care what my logical mind says. These are matters of the heart.

As the singer coos about how things are always better when we're together, I lean my head softly on Sean's shoulder. He wraps me even tighter in his embrace and continues to move us with the soothing beat. I close my eyes, in absolute heaven.

Tenderly, Sean begins to sing along to the lyrics, kissing my forehead in between lines. He has an incredible voice. It's a rich baritone, and it sounds like warmth and contentment. I swoon some more at being the object of this man's affection. I'm one lucky lady right now.

How did I get so lucky? But who cares how? Just go with it.

I feel the rumble in Sean's chest as he sings, his body an instrument. I'm certain I could listen to his voice for the rest of my days. Now I understand why he's traveling with a guitar. Anyone who sounds this amazing should be singing every chance he gets.

I let myself dream. I soak it all up, allowing visions of a big, jolly future to take over.

I see us together as the years and seasons go by, Sean holding me and quietly singing to me. I see us on the beach. I see us at summer picnics and social gatherings. I see us in fall foliage, in the snow of Tennessee winters, and everywhere in between. I see Sean down on one knee with his guitar, asking for my hand in marriage. I can't help it. I see him standing at an altar with the ocean in the background. And I see him singing softly as he rocks our infant to sleep.

It's as if I'm seeing into our future. As if it's all a certainty.

Whoa.

I jerk my eyes open. That was too much.

I mean, it wasn't too much for *me*. I hate to admit that to myself. But it wasn't. Not really. Sean and I together feel right as rain. But I don't want to scare the guy off. And I don't want to set myself up for heartbreak and disappointment. I barely know him.

I sound like a crazy person.

I know.

"Daydreaming?" Sean asks as I lift my head.

The song ends and I work to collect my thoughts, forcing my attention to the public setting around me. I shake my head, as if to shake off the daydream and ground myself.

"Something like that," I reply, pulling back from Sean's embrace and smoothing my shirt. "We had better get moving if we want to shop, eat, swim, and be back at the airport on time."

"Whatever you say," Sean says. "You're the boss."

His tone isn't sarcastic, but rather like he's ready to make my every wish come true.

I've always been a sucker for the whole fairy-tale love thing. At least, a modern version of it. No one knows that except my closest friends, and I have a hard time admitting it to them, let alone to myself. I want to be romanced. I want to be swept off my feet. And I want to feel like my man's one and only. Like he has eyes for me and me alone.

Sean is stirring up all of that longing. He's putting things into my head that I had nearly given up on.

What's a girl to do?

We proceed to the swim shop down the block. The walk is quick, and the store isn't busy when we arrive. A perky woman with blonde hair and red lips much like our flight attendant's greets us with a friendly smile. I tell her what I'm looking for and she points me in the right direction.

Sean was right again. The shop has everything I need.

I select a swimsuit that's sexier than anything I've ever worn before. Rosalie and Ella would be proud. It's white with peach, baby blue, and taupe floral print, a one piece featuring a plunging v-neckline and low scoop back. Halter straps cross between my shoulder blades and wrap around my body. I feel sweet and pretty, while at the same time oh, so desirable. It suits me ... pun intended. I choose it without even trying anything else.

Maybe Sean will use the straps to unwrap me like a present.

Hope so.

I also find a halter-top maxi dress in a sea glass blue color that coordinates and fits just right over top of the swimsuit. I pair the look with strappy, heeled sandals and a wide brim hat. My gold hoop earrings coordinate just fine. It's all perfect.

I take a few extra minutes in the dressing room to reapply my makeup and lip gloss.

Now I'm ready for South Beach.

Bring it, Miami.

Sean whistles loudly when I step out wearing my new outfit. He has changed into a short-sleeve shirt that shows off his muscular physique. He looks hot as hell.

"Va-va-va-voom," he blurts, grinning from ear to ear.

I'm not sure who says that anymore, but it sounds sexy coming from him.

I blush. And I laugh.

"Good?" I ask, already knowing the answer.

Sean moves close and scoops me into his arms, then

plants a warm kiss on my lips. "You're the most beautiful woman in the world, Darling. I'm glad we've finally found each other."

I go weak in the knees. He practically has to pick me up off the floor. I tell you, I'm smitten.

Smitten!

CHAPTER 10

SEAN

The warm Miami sun casts a golden glow over Clara's face as we walk along the vibrant shops of South Beach.

Her excitement is palpable, evident in the way she fiddles with the straps of her newly purchased swimsuit with a mischievous sparkle in her eyes. She's itching to show it off, and truth be told, I'm itching to see her in it. I can't help but feel my pulse quicken as my gaze travels down her figure, imagining how stunning she'll look in that swimwear.

As we stroll, her radiant smile draws the attention of passersby, and I can't help but feel a surge of pride. Clara is a sight to behold—a vibrant, confident woman who exudes a magnetic energy. And with every step, my attraction to her intensifies.

Clara sidesteps a couple browsing a rack of beach towels and turns her gaze towards me. "So, Sean," she begins, her voice laced with curiosity, "we've been working together for a while now, but I realize I know next to nothing about your personal life. Tell me, where do you come from? Who's in your family?"

I match her playful tone, leaning in slightly. "Ah, Clara, you've uncovered my secrets. Well, hold on tight, because you're about to get a glimpse into the enigma that is Sean O'Shea." I pause, drawing out the suspense before continuing. "Actually, I'll get to that, but I'd like to hear more about you first."

Her eyes widen, a mix of surprise and intrigue. "Me? There isn't much to tell. At least, that's my story, and I'm sticking to it."

Her laughter rings through the air, and I find myself captivated by the melody. She's more than just a beautiful woman—I'm drawn to her spirit, and her wit.

The attraction between us becomes palpable, and with every step, the tension grows. Hell, the tension isn't the only thing that's growing. My shorts are incredibly tight right now.

Oof.

We pause in front of a café, the aroma of freshly brewed coffee wafting through the air.

"You know, Darling," I say, "I have a feeling there's much more to you than meets the eye. Behind that smile, I sense a depth that intrigues me."

"Well," she replies, "I don't know about that."

"Why are you deflecting?" I ask, genuinely curious.

I don't mean it as a criticism.

She hems and haws a bit, then gets brutally honest. "It's been a while since I've gone on a date. I feel out of practice."

I chuckle, my eyes twinkling with mischief. "Who

said anything about dating? We're just two friends enjoying each other's company, right?"

She raises an eyebrow, a playful smirk curling her lips. "Oh, is that how you see it? Just friends, huh?"

I lean closer. "Exactly. No pressure, no expectations. Just two people exploring South Beach, getting to know each other."

Clara's laughter fills the air, the sound like music to my ears. We come to a stop in front of a cozy book shop, and I motion for us to sit at one of the benches out front. We settle in, the vibrant energy of the bustling street surrounding us.

She rests her hand beside her on the bench, her gaze meeting mine. "You're a smooth talker, Sean. But tell me, what else would you like to know about me?"

I lean back, watching the people walk by, contemplating her question. "I want to know everything. The big and the small, the dreams and the fears. I want to know the real *you*."

A flicker of hesitation passes through her eyes, and for a moment, she seems lost in thought. "I suppose you could say I'm a bit guarded when it comes to my personal life."

I nod, sensing there's more beneath the surface. "No worries. We all have our reasons for holding back. But when you're ready, I'll be here, eager to listen."

She smiles appreciatively, a softness in her eyes that tugs at my heartstrings. "Thank you, Sean. It means a lot to have someone willing to listen without judgment."

Curiosity gnaws at me, wanting to uncover the layers she's hidden away. What judgment has she experienced? I decide to change the subject to something lighter. Something easier for her to talk about.

"So, tell me about your best friends, Rosie and Ella. What's the story there?" I ask. "You three were friends as kids, right?"

Clara's face lights up, and a spark of joy dances in her eyes. "Rosie and Ella are my rocks, my partners in crime. We've been friends since forever. Through thick and thin, they've always had my back."

I lean in, my voice low and intimate. "And what about your family, Clara? I'd love to know more about where you come from."

So much for something lighter. I can't seem to help myself. I want to get to what's real.

Clara hesitates, her fingers tracing the seam of her dress. "My parents and my childhood ... it's a bit complicated. Let's just say I grew up in Loveland, and leave it at that for now."

I sense her deflection, her desire to keep a part of herself hidden. I know that trust takes time. But damn.

"Okay, there's plenty of time, Clara," I say softly, my eyes locked with hers. "We're just scratching the surface. Sorry if I'm moving too fast."

A flicker of relief crosses her face, and a gentle smile plays on her lips. "Thank you, but I never said we're moving too fast. I might like to move things faster in some regards ... if you know what I mean."

She scoots closer and raises her dress, exposing a few more inches of delicious thigh for my viewing pleasure. And now my shorts are definitely constraining my ... goods.

Ouch. But in a good way.

I clear my throat and tell myself to focus. "Darling," I say, my voice laced with sincerity, "I want you to know that I'm here for whatever pace you're comfortable with. But I can't deny the attraction that sizzles between us. You feel it too, right?"

She tilts her head, a hint of mischief dancing in her eyes. "Oh, Sean, are you suggesting we *could* move fast? Rosie and Ella have been encouraging me to be open to a little adventure. I think they'd approve of … whatever you have in mind."

I feel a surge of heat rush through my veins as her words hang in the air. The image of her exposed leg, a tantalizing glimpse of what could be, stirs an undeniable desire within me. I take a deep breath, gathering my thoughts before responding.

I lean close and can feel the heat radiating from her neck. It drives me wild. "There's no denying the chemistry between us," I confess, my voice low and husky. "But before we dive headfirst into the deep end, I need to know if you'd be comfortable with that. If you'd be comfortable kissing me and perhaps … doing more."

She leans even closer, her voice a breathy whisper. "I'm comfortable."

My heart races in my chest as her words send a surge of desire through me. The air around us becomes charged with an electric tension, and I find myself unable to resist the magnetic pull drawing me closer to her.

We continue our flirtatious banter, our words laced with innuendo and suggestion. The heat between us builds with each passing moment, our playful exchange creating a symphony of desire. But before things can escalate further, we decide it's time to regain our composure.

Clara smirks, her eyes glinting with a mixture of anticipation and mischief. "As much as I'd love to explore every inch of South Beach with you, Sean, I think we should find a place to grab some lunch. A little sustenance before our swim at the beach."

I chuckle, a mix of relief and longing flooding my senses. "You're right. Food might be the best way to channel our energies for now. But I must warn you, I might need to find a clever way to hide a certain ... physical reaction."

She raises an eyebrow, a playful glimmer in her eyes. "Is that so? I'll be watching closely to see just how well you can hide it."

With a laugh, we rise from the bench, our bodies just inches apart. The electric charge between us remains, a reminder of what awaits beneath the surface. For now, we tame the flames of desire, focusing on the simple pleasure of good company.

As we walk hand in hand, searching for the perfect lunch spot, I can't help but wonder what lies ahead. Our connection is undeniable, and the chemistry that courses through my veins urges me to explore every facet of Clara. But I also realize that building a foundation, deepening our bond beyond the physical, is just as crucial.

So, we venture forth, eager to savor the delights of both nourishment and companionship. Our bodies may hunger for more, but for now, we will feast on laughter and conversation.

As we step into a nearby restaurant to get a table, I steal a glance at Clara.

Damn, that woman is something else. I'd like to make her mine.

CHAPTER 11

CLARA

"So, tell me about yourself," I prompt between bites of cheeseburger.

We're sitting in an outdoor dining area under a chic white umbrella with a view of the Atlantic in the distance. It seems like a reasonable question. I've heard bits and pieces about Sean peppered in between small talk, but I should probably know more about the man I'm now imagining a future with.

It's funny though, because I feel like the details aren't really all that significant. Again, I know I sound like a crazy person.

I know!

"Where should I start?" Sean asks jovially as he pops a handful of crisp, golden french fries into his mouth.

Cheeseburger in paradise.

Jimmy Buffet was onto something. Now I understand the appeal.

This food is tasty.

"How about you start with where you're from. And where you live. That kind of thing," I say.

"Okay," Sean mumbles as he chews. "Well, I'm from Boston …"

"I knew it!" I exclaim. "I thought I heard a Massachusetts accent."

"Good catch," he says. He chuckles, enjoying the playful banter. "I do my best to live up to the hard-working, gritty, loyal-to-a-fault stereotype. But don't let the accent fool you. There's more to me than that."

I raise an eyebrow, a teasing smile playing on my lips. "Oh, really? "Go on."

"I recently relocated to a little town in Tennessee. It's not far from Nashville, yet it feels a world away. I've only been there a few months. I'm digging it."

Digging it?

He's starting to seem like a dork with all these old-school phrases.

An adorable dork.

"Oh?" I ask. "Sounds like my neck of the woods. What's the name of the town?"

Say Loveland. Say Loveland.

SAY LOVELAND!

"Loveland."

I almost choke on my food. I knew he'd come to Loveland to film the docu-series, but I didn't know he *lived* there. Or had any intention of staying there.

"Are you serious?" I ask, slurping down a drink of my local beer to keep from coughing up my lunch. "You *live* there."

I'm drinking Islamorada Ale. And yes, we're day drinking. Why not?

"Yeah, why wouldn't I be serious?" he asks.

"Because that's where I live. It's where I'm from. Born and raised."

"No way!" Sean exclaims as he stands up, leans across the table, and kisses me again. Deeply this time.

He knows I live there. He's being dramatic. Or silly. Or something fun.

"Yeah, what are the odds?" I ask, rhetorically.

"I'm beginning to think there's something larger at work here," Sean muses. "Are you my destiny, Clara Darling?"

"Maybe," I say, unable to hide my glee.

This is incredible news. How did it take us this long to figure it out? Sean living in Loveland is almost impossible to believe. It's everything to me. I imagined him staying in a weekly-rent hotel with a couple of bags of clothes. This is entirely different.

"I'm stoked," Sean adds. "We can see each other more when we get home. Outside of work."

I raise my eyebrows.

"If you want to … I don't mean to be … presumptuous …"

"Of course, we can see each other more when we get home … outside of work," I reply. "I'd love that."

"Oh, Darling," Sean replies. "Please don't be offended when I can't suggest fun things to do, though. I've had my head buried in work."

"What do you do?"

"That's a great story," he says, chomping on more

french fries. He's teasing again. I know he is a cameraman working on the docu-series. "Call me loony," he muses, "but I bought a farm."

"A farm?" My eyeballs practically pop out of my head.

"Yep. Out on Highway 46. The old Jenkins place. I'm turning it into a fruit and fir farm. Apples, berries, peaches, pumpkins, and Christmas trees. Maybe even a vineyard with a winery at some point. I'd love to give Kix Brooks and Arrington Vineyards a little friendly competition."

"Are you serious right now?" I ask again.

"Completely. Getting the farm off the ground has been a dream of mine for quite a while. My parents struggled when I was a kid. They were at work all the time. My grandfather practically raised me. Well, him and my Uncle Finn. I have the best memories of picking fruit with them in the summer and fall, and of cutting our own Christmas trees in the winter. Classic childhood stuff. I want to be surrounded by that kind of simple happiness every day. I plan to open a farmer's market and create activities for families to enjoy together. You know, corn mazes, hay rides and sleigh rides. That kind of thing."

"Aww," I say.

"Yeah, you'll find out I'm a big softie at heart," he adds. "Don't let this tough, strong exterior fool you."

I tilt my head, my eyes gleaming with genuine interest. "And what about your background? Any hidden family secrets or international connections?"

He winks at me, allowing a hint of mystery to color

his response. "Well, I do have a little international flavor in my blood. My grandfather is from Ireland, emigrated to the States when Dad and Uncle Finn were kids. So, I've got a touch of the Irish charm running through my veins."

I playfully nudge him with my elbow. "I knew there was something about you that made me weak in the knees."

We catch our breath, the proximity between us suddenly sparking an electric charge.

"Careful there, Darling," Sean says. "You might unleash the full extent of this Irish charm. I can't be held responsible for the consequences."

We laugh together. It feels good.

"So why Loveland?"

"I don't know. Maybe so I could meet you."

I blush even more. I can feel the heat in my cheeks. I'd love for what he's saying to be true. I'd be thrilled for there to be some cosmic plan that insists we be together.

"Aww," I manage.

My vocabulary becomes limited when I'm flustered.

"But before I knew about you, I picked Loveland for its quaint charm and close proximity to Music City. It seemed like a good place to stake my claim. I know just enough to be dangerous with marketing. My plan is to lure harried city dwellers from their high rises and tall skinnies for some family time in a place with fresh air and open spaces."

"Sounds like a plan that could work," I confirm. "I

own a travel agency, and I can tell you firsthand that Loveland is becoming a sought-after destination."

"Darling, you own a travel agency, of all things, yeah?"

"I do."

"And you'd never been on a plane before today …"

"Well … I … Wait. I never told you that," I mutter.

Sean laughs and takes another bite of his burger, onions and pickles threatening to ooze over the side. When he's done chewing, he reaches across the table and takes my hand.

"Don't be mad at me for saying this, but I could tell."

I laugh out loud now, tipping my head back and holding my bouncing belly. Sean joins me. It's funny. I know it is.

"Mad?" I ask. "I was a hot mess on that plane. I can hardly pretend I wasn't. I'm not mad. Thank you for being so sweet to me."

He runs his thumb gently over the top of my hand.

"I'm glad I was there. Glad I could comfort you in your time of need."

"Me, too."

We sit quietly for a few minutes, eating our food while holding hands and enjoying the ocean breeze. I love that we can be at ease together without words. The silence is just as comfortable as our conversation.

"I guess I should tell you something else about me," Sean adds. "About what I did before the farm … And what I still do …"

"Okay," I reply.

I wonder why he's acting strange about it, whatever it is.

"I'm a songwriter."

"Okay, nice," I reply. "And you mentioned that on the plane, remember?" He nods. "You're an amazing singer," I continue. "I can totally see it. I'll bet you're amazing on guitar as well."

"Thanks," he says. "I'm afforded more anonymity than the stars who sing my songs. Thank goodness."

He pauses, like he's trying to find the right words.

"You can tell me anything," I assure. "Go ahead."

"Okay. I just don't want to come across as self important. It's not what I'm about. But in between Boston and Loveland, I lived in Los Angeles. And my songwriting has been quite a success. I've written songs for many of the artists you probably know. I've been at it for nearly a decade."

"Wow!" I say, trying not to sound like a fan girl.

"Yeah, but I'm not into the lifestyle of glitz and glam that many people in this industry seek. I'm about the lyrics. You know, the soul of a song. I don't need a fancy house or expensive car to go along with them. I'd rather be picking the strings while I look out over my farm in small-town Tennessee than doing so while sitting in a fancy house in California. And besides, I wanted to get my farm going while my grandpa is still around to see it. I'm bringing him down to live with me in Loveland just as soon as I get a place ready."

"Aww," I mumble again.

I can't help it. All indications prove that this man is tailor made for me.

"But don't get me wrong," he adds, stroking my hand again. "For the right woman, I'll do anything. Go anywhere. As long as Grandpa is taken care of and the rest of the family is alright. We can travel. I don't mean to imply that we'd be stuck on the farm."

There is a we. Holy hell.

"That's sweet," I say, flustered again.

"I earned a nice share of royalties over the years, and I have a nest egg," Sean continues. "I intend to hire staff to manage the farm. I travel now and then to play with my artist friends. It's fun. No one knows me, but I get on stage and play for my own enjoyment. I'd like to keep that up."

"Is that why you're going to the Cayman Islands with a guitar on your back?"

He chuckles.

"It is. Buck is playing a concert there in a few days. He invited me down to join in."

"Buck?" I ask. "As in Buck Davenport, the famous country artist?"

"That's the one. He's partial to Caribbean islands. Stays down there as much as he can."

"You know, I heard that somewhere," I reply, still trying not to sound like a fangirl.

Everyone has heard that about Buck Davenport, haven't they? So many of his songs are about the beach and the islands. I think he has a house on Saint John, in the Virgin Islands.

"Yeah?" Sean asks.

"Yeah."

I grin at him, imagining him on stage at Rosie's party

last night, and I can't help but wonder if he has aspirations that go beyond writing songs for other artists. He's good on stage. I saw that for myself.

I decide to keep those thoughts to myself, for the time being.

"Well, enough about me. Tell me all about you," Sean says, then grabs the last few fries on his plate and puts them into his mouth.

Before I can answer, both of our phones buzz at the same time. We look down at the alerts at the same time. It's an update from the airline. There's been a four-hour delay. Our quick trip to the beach just got a lot more leisurely.

We smile up at each other.

"The airline?" I ask.

"Yep. Flight to Grand Cayman delayed?"

"Yep."

Thinking the same thing at the same time, we lean across the table and share a lingering kiss. It's South Beach. Nobody cares.

"Time for swimming?" I ask.

"You mean, time for me to see that sexy body in all its swimsuit-clad glory? Then, yes. Finish your cheeseburger, then I'm more than ready."

I blush, redder and hotter than ever.

CHAPTER 12

SEAN

Sitting at the warm metal dining table on the patio, I watch as Clara takes another bite of her cheeseburger, her eyes lighting up with delight. The distant view of the Atlantic Ocean serves as a picturesque backdrop, amplifying the magic of the moment.

A stray dog meanders towards our table, hopeful eyes peering up at us.

I can't help but smile at Clara's immediate affinity for the furry visitor. She extends her hand, petting the dog's head with tenderness. The sight warms my heart, further solidifying my feelings for her.

The pup has long black fur and a thin nose. He looks to me like some sort of collie mix. He's a handsome guy, his silky coat shimmering in the sun. He isn't wearing a collar. Although, he appears well fed for a stray.

"Looks like we've got an unexpected guest," I remark, amusement lacing my voice.

Clara chuckles, her laughter like music to my ears, as

always. "Seems like it. You know, I've always wanted to be a dog person."

I lean back in my chair, intrigued by her response. "Really? Wanted to be? I take it that means you don't have a dog now. What kind would you choose if you had the chance?"

She takes a moment, her gaze drifting as she visualizes the dog of her dreams. "I've always had a soft spot for sheepadoodles. They're beautiful and intelligent. If I had one, I'd name her Caroline, so that I could sing Sweet Caroline and teach her to somehow do the bum, bum, bum part."

"Huh," I say. "Nice choice. Maybe she can tap her little paw on the ground three times."

We both laugh.

The image of Clara with a fluffy sheepadoodle by her side brings a warmth to my chest. "Caroline. That's a wonderful name. She'd be lucky to have you as her owner."

A blush tinges Clara's cheeks, and my heart swells with affection. "Thank you. But truth be told, I've never had a dog before. I'm not sure if I'd know how to handle one."

I lean forward. "I think you underestimate yourself. Handling a dog is something you learn as you go. And if you ever need any help or guidance, I'll be right there with you. I grew up with dogs. They're practically a part of my DNA."

Her eyes fill with gratitude, and a soft smile graces her lips. "That means a lot to me, Sean. Your support and knowledge would make all the difference. Maybe

Caroline wouldn't be such a daunting challenge after all. Sometimes I think maybe I should start with a smaller breed, but I really want a sheepadoodle. A big, fluffy, lovable sheepadoodle."

"The woman knows what she wants," I say with a smile. "I like that."

As our conversation continues, our thoughts begin to dance towards the future. Maybe it's something about being in this exotic city that's creating an ambiance of hope and endless possibilities. Anything and everything is fair game.

We're adventurers. Dreamers. Lovers.

"You know," I say, my voice filled with a mix of conviction and longing, "I've always envisioned myself with a family. I imagine kids running around, and laughter filling the house."

A flicker of emotion passes through Clara's eyes, her vulnerability apparent. "I've had those dreams, too," she confesses, her voice barely above a whisper. "A home where love flourishes, where we create memories together. Much like what Rosie and Patrick are building, beginning with their new pup, Penny. Did you see her at the party last night? She is the absolute cutest."

"Yeah?" I say. "I saw her, but I didn't have a chance to hold or pet her. That's on my to-do list for when we return home. Are you saying you want a puppy, Darling? Should I get you one?"

She tucks her chin against her chest and looks up at me with pleading eyes. "Maybe. I suppose it depends on how things go for us on this trip, right?"

In that moment, the weight of her words settles deep

within me, anchoring me to a future I had only dared to dream about. Clara Darling has captured my soul in a way I never expected.

"Darling," I say, my voice filled with unwavering certainty, "whatever the future holds, I want you by my side. I want to share it all with you—the laughter, the challenges, the beautiful moments that make life worth living."

Her eyes meet mine, her vulnerability mingling with a newfound sense of hope. "Sean, I feel the same way. With you, I see a future filled with love and joy. I think we could build something remarkable together."

The air crackles with anticipation, the promise of a shared journey unfolding before us. Our words hang in the warm breeze, intertwining with the rhythm of the crowd shuffling on the street nearby.

The dog inches closer, catching a whiff of the food left on Clara's plate.

Her face lights up with a mixture of surprise and affection as she reaches out to pet the pup. "Well, hello there, sweetie. Aren't you a handsome fellow?"

His tail wags even more vigorously as Clara scratches behind his ears.

"She has a way with animals," I say, unable to hide my admiration. "That much is obvious."

Clara looks up at me, a sparkle of joy in her eyes. "Animals bring out the best in people, don't you think? They have this way of connecting with our hearts."

I nod, a smile tugging at the corners of my lips. "Absolutely. They have an incredible ability to show unconditional love and bring a sense of joy into our lives."

As Clara continues to shower the pooch with affection, she turns her attention back to me. "You know, Sean, I've always admired people who are good with animals. It says a lot about their character."

I meet her gaze, a tinge of pride seeping into my voice. "Are you asking if you can trust me? Because you can. I hope you know that by now. I'd never let anything happen to you."

As Clara's blush deepens, a mix of hope and uncertainty fills her eyes. She takes a moment, her gaze searching mine, and a question hangs in the air. "Sean, building a future together requires trust. Can I trust you?"

I meet her gaze, the sincerity in her question not lost on me. I reach out, gently cupping her cheek. "Darling, trust is the foundation of any relationship. I want you to know that you can trust me with your heart, your dreams, and your fears. I'm here for you, through the ups and downs, and I will always be honest and true."

"Okay, but you kind of sound like a guy out of a Nicholas Sparks movie right now. Do you hear yourself?" she asks.

"So, what? What I'm telling you is true." I say.

A flicker of relief passes through Clara's eyes, her vulnerability slowly melting away. "Okay. Thank you, Sean. I believe you, and I want to take this journey with you."

I smile, the weight of her words lifting from my shoulders. "I'm honored, Clara. Together, we'll create a bond built on trust, respect, and unwavering support. We'll face any challenges that come our way, hand in hand."

The collie, sensing the change in the atmosphere, lifts its head and nuzzles Clara's hand, as if to offer reassurance of its own. We share a laugh, basking in the warmth of the sun and the newfound connection between us.

I make a mental note to dig deeper, as soon as possible. This woman has been hurt. I need to find out how and why so that I can help her heal.

When I'm sure she's all done eating, it's time to move on to the next part of our Miami adventure.

"Shall we, Clara?" I offer, extending my hand towards her.

I pay the check and we step into the bright South Florida sun, hand in hand, then head for the brilliant blue waters that beckon us. There will be plenty of time for Clara to tell me more about herself. Later.

I can't wait to get my hands on this woman up close and personal as the silky warm water surrounds us. I want to check out her round chest and his toned legs. And if I play my cards right, maybe I'll get a chance to feel them pressed up against me, skin to skin, too.

She accepts, her fingers interlacing with mine, and we rise from our seats. The collie, sensing our departure, rises as well, wagging its tail as if bidding us farewell.

The future holds infinite possibilities, and as we prepare to dive into the unknown, I can't wait to see where this adventure leads us.

The dog, sensing our attention shift away, releases a contented sigh and plops down on the ground beside us. Clara chuckles, her eyes lingering on the dog. "Looks like we've made a new friend."

I grin, my heart swelling with affection for both Clara and the pup. "Seems like it. Perhaps this furry encounter is a sign of the good things to come."

"Maybe we should give him a name," she says. "To remember him by, at least."

"Okay then," I say. "What should we call him?"

"Arnold," she replies, as if she's been thinking about it for a while.

"Like Schwarzenegger?" I ask with a laugh.

"Yeah, so?"

I smile broadly. "Arnold it is."

CHAPTER 13

CLARA

I'm waiting outside a public changing room for Sean to put his swimming trunks on when I decide I have to get in touch with Rosalie and Ella. This is too good to keep from them a moment longer, and besides, they'll be expecting me to land in Grand Cayman in a few hours. They might worry if I don't tell them about the delay.

It's funny, a little while ago, I was thinking about how I might lose out on a night of my scheduled hotel reservation and incur additional change fees. I've loosened up tremendously as the day has gone on. I've decided that money isn't any good without a reason to enjoy it. I've worked hard. It's time to reap some of the rewards. And if we're delayed ... then whatever. I don't much care where I am, as long as Sean and I are together.

I pull my dress off over my head and tuck it into my bag. I feel good in my new swimsuit. I feel sexy.

The sun is warm on my skin.

I forgot to pick up sunscreen, but think I'll probably be okay without it as long as I keep my hat on. I have my African-American dad to thank for those genetics. My pale mom burns like a lobster.

Ella picks up on the first ring, her gravelly Long Island mobster voice familiar in my ear.

"Hello?" she says as if she doesn't know who it is.

My number shows up on her smartphone's caller ID, complete with a photo of my smiling face. She knows who it is.

"Hey," I say. "Get Rosalie! Quick. I only have a few minutes."

"Right-o," Ella barks, then disappears until Rosalie's line begins to ring.

"Yes? What's up?" Rosalie asks, thinking it's only Ella.

"We've got Clara on the line," Ella says. "She has to make it fast."

"Okay," Rosalie confirms. "Does she want us to check in with Matt to find out how the travel agency is doing without her?"

Matt Sellinger is my new hire, a group sales guy who helps out with general business management. He's in charge while I'm away.

"Hey," I say again. "Forget about Matt. Listen up, ladies... I met someone."

"Oh, how fabulous!" Rosalie says.

"Nice," Ella adds. "Who? How?"

"Sean O'Shea. I'm waiting for him to change into swimming trunks as we speak. We're at South Beach in Miami."

"What??" my friends ask in unison. They sound as shocked as I feel.

"Long story. I'm sending you a picture of us together. Of our first kiss."

"Whoo wee," Ella exclaims. "You work fast."

"Wow!" Rosalie echoes. "Did you shave this morning?"

"What kind of question is that?" I ask with a laugh. "Yes, I shaved this morning. Isn't that part of the customary prep process when flying to the tropics?"

"Phew," Rosalie laughs back. "So, you're all set."

Ella chuckles too.

"I'll explain more later," I say as fast as I can. Time is running out. "My flight to Grand Cayman is delayed. Sean's on that flight too. We're about to get into the ocean … and I suspect the heat level is about to increase, if you know what I mean."

Ella laughs. "We know what you mean. You're always so straight laced, Clara. Loosen up. You're allowed to live a little."

"Really? You think so?" I ask. "Because, you know how I am. This is way out of my comfort zone."

"Definitely," Rosalie confirms. "Trust your gut. If it tells you to go for it, then go for it! You're a grown woman. And a smart, successful, attractive one at that. Do what you want, my dear."

"Okay! Thanks, you two. I gotta go. He's coming."

They squeal into the phone. It's our rowdy party routine.

"Coming is good," Ella manages to add before I press the red button to end the call.

Coming is good.

As he saunters in my direction, Sean looks at me knowingly. He has stripped down to nothing but swim trunks now. His body is every bit as sexy as I imagined. He's staring at me. Hard.

A quick glance at his trunks tells me something else is hard.

Oh, my God.

"Let me guess. Rosalie and Ella?" he asks, looking me up and down like I'm a piece of fresh meat. And I don't mean that in a bad way.

"Guilty as charged," I say. "I wanted to make sure they knew about the flight delay. They might have worried."

"Um hmm," he mutters, leaning close and slowly nibbling on one of my earlobes. "Did you tell them about me?"

"Maybe," I say, my loins suddenly alight with desire at his touch.

"Good things?"

"Maybe."

He nibbles again.

"Send them our picture?"

"Not yet."

He takes more of my earlobe into his mouth, one hand grazing slowly across my nipples as he wraps his arm around the front of me. They stand at attention. Perky. Ready for more of his attention. The fabric of my swimsuit is paper thin.

Now I'm done for.

Sean might as well penetrate me right here on the

sand in front of all these people. My body aches for him. It's an ache so primal, so all encompassing that I don't think I could resist him if I tried. I've never felt like this about a man. It's as if the others were all just boys, incapable of actually meeting my needs.

This blossoming relationship is a grown-up one. It's real. I know it is.

"Take another picture," he says, still nibbling.

"What this time?"

"Our first swim together." Nibble. "Our first time at the beach together." Nibble. "Our first day spent together."

Nibble. Suck. Nibble.

He moves his hand back across my now rock-hard and ultra-sensitive nipples, lingering even longer at each one and giving them a gentle twist between his knuckles.

This man is a skilled and attentive lover. I can tell that much for sure.

I want him to ravage me.

"All of that?" I ask, hardly able to speak. My eyes close and roll up in my head in response to the pleasure my body is feeling.

He moves down from my earlobe and buries his face into my neck, nibbling and sucking in all the right places.

"All of that," he confirms between hot breaths. "And the two of us, falling in love."

His woodsy-coconut scent wafts through the air and tickles my nose.

This feels amazing. It IS amazing.

I raise my phone to take the picture.

Click.

He doesn't move from my neck.

"Is that what we're doing?" I ask. "Falling in love?"

Click.

"You tell me," he says, moving up to my lips inch by inch, making me wild with desire.

Click.

I continue taking photos.

"I don't know," I say. "But you had better take it easy, unless you intend to have me right here on this beach. You'll push me past the point of no return, if you aren't careful."

"Will I, now?" he asks in the most sexy growl I've ever heard.

He pushes me playfully behind the concrete wall of the changing rooms, out of sight. I cooperate, leaning back against the cool blocks in a seductive stance with one arm up above my head. I let my bag fall to the ground, feeling the sand between my toes as my sandals sink deep.

I know what else I'd like to sink deep. Gracious!

Sean sets his guitar case nearby. He doesn't have another bag, so apparently keeps his clothes and personal items inside with his instrument. Whatever. I like that he travels light. It adds to his carefree and whimsical persona.

He moves towards me in a slow saunter, pausing just inches away from my face before continuing. He means to make sure this is a real connection. And I feel it. We stare into each other's eyes, transfixed. Every cell in my body wants this man. This life. We're a matched set. Two parts of one whole.

I don't care if we haven't known each other long. I suspect we've been waiting all of our lives to do so.

Hungrily, I reach out and grab him by the biceps. I can't wait a minute longer. I pull him to me, fumbling with the drawstring on his trunks as he slides a hand between my legs.

I'm dripping wet for him, my sensitive bud throbbing with every beat of my heart. He touches it with a firm finger, and I nearly burst in an instant.

But I don't want to release yet. I tell myself to hold it in. To wait.

I want to feel him inside of me.

Our mouths find each other and kiss deeply. Our tongues intertwine as our hands explore. Gripping and grasping, we cover every important corner of each other.

Sean presses against me hard and I feel his firm manhood. It's eager for me. And it's big. Massive, actually. For a second, I wonder if I can handle it.

Nonsense. Of course, I can.

I enjoy being desired. It heightens my level of arousal even more. And I've never felt as desired as I do right now.

Sean cups my wetness in his hand, expertly working his way around my folds and sending pulses of pleasure like bolts of lightning throughout my body. My entire being feels electrified. On fire.

"Ooh," I moan with delight.

He leans down to my bosom and uses his teeth to

pull my swimsuit to one side, exposing one breast. With just the right amount of pressure, he licks my nipple, moving his mouth around it in a slow, circular motion.

The warm air feels exquisite. Sean feels exquisite. Everything feels exquisite.

I caress the back of his head with one hand as he continues to mouth my nipple, my fingers wiggling through his short hair. He keeps his other hand between my legs, rubbing expertly as he takes me to new heights.

I swear, I've never felt like this before. Certainly not with Benton. Not with Roy. Not even with Michael. I didn't know this level of pleasure existed.

I moan more. I can't help myself. I stand on my tip toes as Sean works me over, rubbing, licking, and pleasing me in all sorts of ways. I lean against the concrete blocks, my eyes still closed. I don't care if anyone sees us. At this point, I'm pretty sure I'd let an audience watch. I am completely and utterly oblivious to everything else.

These are the best moments.

"Wait," Sean says, suddenly pulling back. He takes his hand away and I ache.

I moan again, disgruntled this time.

Dammit.

"Don't go," I plead, reluctantly opening my eyes. "I want you."

Sean shakes his head, "I want you too, Darling. But this is important. I should romance you. Our first time can't be like this."

"Why not?" I ask, impatiently.

While I appreciate Sean's sentiment, I don't want to wait. I want him now.

Now, now, now.

"You've been romancing me all day."

He raises one hand and tugs on his hair. I practically mew like a kitty with desire just looking at him. I'm the very definition of hot and bothered right now.

Sean stays quiet for a moment, thinking.

"Let's get in the water," he says.

CHAPTER 14

CLARA

This man is killing me. Not literally, of course.

But damn.

Before I can object, Sean picks up our things and grabs me by the hand, leading me to the water's edge. He drops our bags hastily as we make our way into the sparkling blue expanse. Seagulls circle overhead as the rhythmic sounds of the waves beckon us to go deeper.

I want Sean to go deeper.

Maybe I'll make a concerted effort to seduce him, right here and now. Maybe he needs some romancing.

I've never made love in the ocean before, but I'd like to today. I suddenly have a one track mind. Like a horny teenager. I want Sean inside of me. Right away.

Now, now, now.

I read in a magazine somewhere that thinking of boring things like tires or trash receptacles can help delay orgasm. I do my best to follow that guidance, conjuring images of auto parts, trash cans, and cleaning supplies. Anything to take my mind off of sexy time long enough to get Sean in the mood again.

It works. Sort of.

At least, temporarily.

As I submerge myself into the Atlantic little by little, I'm dazzled by the warmth of the water and how silky it feels.

"Like bath water," I mutter.

Still holding my hand, Sean turns and smiles. "Yeah?"

"It's different from the beaches up north where my parents like to vacation, that's for sure," I add. "And the water is so clear. I can see all the way to the bottom!"

"It is pretty great," he confirms. "We should go snorkeling when we get to Grand Cayman. Just wait until you see all the tropical fish swimming in the crystal-clear waters around there. It's something."

I light up when I hear that he wants us to spend time together in Grand Cayman. We hadn't specifically discussed it yet. But now, it's official.

"So, you want us to hang out together when we get to the island?" I ask.

"Absolutely, Darling," he confirms. "Don't you?"

"I definitely do."

He stops, apparently set on a spot about ten feet out from shore where we can park ourselves as we enjoy the water. Windsurfers frolic on top of waves nearby. We have a great view of their colorful sails against the vivid blue sky. I could watch them all day.

"Good," Sean says as he faces me and pulls me towards him. "I think we're on the same page. Right?"

The uncertainty can be paralyzing in a new relationship. I know, because I've been through it. I don't want it to be that way with Sean. It wasn't. Until he pulled away from me back there as I begged for him to stay.

The way it happened is making me feel insecure. And I really, really don't want to seem desperate and insecure. That's never attractive.

"We are on the same page," I reply. "But what was that back there? Why did you pull away?"

I wrap my arms around his neck and press my body against his as we talk. The waves slosh around us, bumping us closer. Sean feels so incredibly good to touch. My perky breasts swell from their place beneath my swimsuit, their roundness on display. My nipples are still hard as a rock. Like the rest of me, they're ready for more stimulation.

Sean sighs. "I didn't want to pull away," he says, leaning his forehead against mine.

"Then why?" I ask again.

"Darling, I'm a man who wants you, I hope that's plain to see. You're gorgeous. And intelligent. And kind. Basically, you're alluring in every possible way. You're the kind of woman I've always wanted to be with. And you rev my engines faster than the ones on the airplane, if you know what I mean."

"Aww."

I melt. And I laugh because I just asked Rosalie and Ella if they knew what I meant about the heat level increasing. Maybe I'm an old-school dork as much as Sean.

Maybe we belong together.

"Va-va-va-voom," he repeats, using his palms to give

my hips a shake. "But I have to also be the man who deserves you. You're a diamond, Darling. You're extra special. And I intend to treat you that way."

"That's sweet," I say. "You're sweet, Sean."

"Well, I'm serious. I want to do this right."

"And you don't think having hot sex on South Beach is doing it right?" I inquire. "Because I gotta admit, that sounds pretty right to me."

"It's just… I don't usually do that kind of thing," Sean explains.

"Sex on the beach?"

"Sex with a woman I just met."

I lean close so my lips are nearly touching his as I talk. There are a dozen or so other swimmers in the vicinity, but none that look like they'll care if we spice things up.

"What's wrong?" I ask, then I kiss him sensually, lingering between phrases. "Do you think we'll be doomed if we make love on the same day we met? Is there an unspoken rule I don't know about? Or a curse?"

My body lights up again as I feel his lips on mine. The fireworks are back.

"You're so silly," he says, kissing me. "No curse that I know of."

"Then why not make love on South Beach today?" I prompt, kissing. *Kissing.* "This is our story. We can make it anything we want."

"And you want sex on South Beach the day we met?" Sean asks as if he doesn't.

But his mouth is against mine. He's kissing. And I

can feel him hardening against me. He wants it. So badly.

"Absolutely," I confirm. "I've never done it before, but I'm willing to try today. We have a beautiful beach here. And technically, we've known each other for weeks on set. Sonny will vouch for you, won't he?"

"Are you sure?" he asks tentatively. "About the sex?"

"Yes, absolutely. Why? Are you worried about the sand? Haven't you ever had sex in the ocean before?"

"I haven't ever had sex on the beach before. Never sex on the beach in South Florida. And never sex on the beach with a woman I just met."

"Never on the beach or in the ocean?" I exclaim. "Seriously? Ever? You're kidding. I thought you were a worldly sort."

"That's the way it is," he confirms. "I've never. How about you?"

"Honey," I say, feeling bold, "I haven't exactly had a lot of sex in my life. Period. Let's just say I've been waiting for someone like you to show up and ... broaden my horizons. Are you up to the task? Because it feels like Junior here is up to something."

I reach down and grab his erection, tracing the line of it with one finger deep between his legs. He doubles over, jumping back, but he doesn't remove his ... *package* ... from my grip.

"Oh, there," he mumbles. "Careful with the family jewels."

I laugh as I roll those jewels between my fingers. "I have nothing but the best intentions, I assure you."

He straightens up, then kisses me deeply.

I'm loving these passionate kisses. I think I've had better kisses this afternoon than the sum today of every single kiss in the past. These are grade A, prime.

"Where'd you learn to kiss like that?" I ask as I draw my bottom lip from between his teeth.

"I think you just inspire me to greatness, Darling," he says, one of his hands cupping my chin and the other sliding to the small of my back.

He leans against me, his member pressing in the perfect spot. I exhale with a burning desire. I want him inside of me. I wasn't kidding. I wasn't unsure. I want him. Right here and now.

"Let's do this," I whisper in his ear as I reach into his swimming trunks and free willy.

He dips a hand between my legs, too, and we moan together, tense with desire. The sun-kissed waves crash against our bodies as we push, pull, and finger each other, creating the most pleasing friction.

Sean's hand is intertwined with mine, his touch sending a current of electricity through my veins. The playful banter and shared laughter have built a bridge of connection, and now, beneath the sunlit waves, I can't help but feel a growing desire for more.

Much, much more. I suspect I'll want it on repeat.

As the water laps at our waists, I turn to face Sean, a sexy smile playing on my lips. "You know, Sean, this beach is known for its warmth. I can't help but wonder if that warmth might extend to something more."

He arches an eyebrow, his eyes dancing with a mixture of intrigue and anticipation. "Are you suggesting we explore the depths of this ocean?"

I laugh, the sound mingling with the crashing waves around us. "Or just the depths of me. The sun, the sea, and your irresistible charm—it's a combination that's hard to resist."

A playful glint flashes in his eyes as he takes a step closer, his voice low and husky. "Well, Darling, if you're willing to brave the currents with me, who am I to deny such a tempting offer? Besides, you already have my dick in your hand. I can't exactly say no without it being awkward."

My heart quickens at his words, my desire growing with each passing second. The warm water caresses our bodies as we move closer, the world around us fading into a blur of anticipation.

His fingers graze the curve of my cheek, sending a shiver of longing down my spine. "Are you sure about this? Once we take that step, there's no turning back."

I meet his gaze, my eyes filled with a fiery determination. "Sean, I've never been more sure about anything in my entire life. I want to dive into this with you, explore the depths of our connection."

A wicked grin spreads across his face, mirroring the intensity that dances within me. "Let's make a splash then, my Darling. Let's show this ocean what we're made of."

With that, our lips crash together, igniting a passionate inferno that engulfs us both. The salty taste of the sea mingles with the sweetness of his kiss, intensifying the sensations that consume us. The waves crash around us, as if echoing the tumultuous desires that surge through our bodies.

As our kiss deepens, the world around us dissolves into a blur of sensations. The ebb and flow of the water match the rhythm of our connection, each wave washing away inhibitions and paving the way for a more profound intimacy.

I reach down and remove my swimsuit bottoms, leaving my lower body free and exposed. It feels glorious, as if the sea and the natural world support the lowering of my inhibitions. I need this, on more than one level.

"There," I say, glancing down at my naked body. No one could tell unless they got close, so I feel fine about it. My breasts are still covered. "Your move, Sean Irish."

He raises his brows, then lifts me in one smooth motion until I'm straddling him, my legs wrapped tightly around his body. Our loins positively ache for one another as he slides inside me and I envelope him, gripping him firmly with my lady muscles.

If Ella were here, she'd make up some bizarre name for the parts and we'd all laugh. Left to my own devices, lady muscles is about the best I can come up with. I did, however, come up with Sean Irish. He seems to like the moniker, too.

"Hey," he says between passionate kisses, "not to distract from the amazing things happening down there, but did you just name me Sean Irish? Because that sounds like the perfect stage name."

We grind against each other as we chat. Honestly, I can't think of a more perfect setting for our first time together. This is absolutely magical. Talk about an adventure!

"I did," I say, "but I didn't think songwriters needed stage names."

"He shrugs playfully. "What if I want to be more than a songwriter? Can you see me on the stage? Or my name on an album cover."

"I can. And now you have your stage name. Glad I could help."

Time loses all meaning as we explore the depths of our desire, our bodies entwined beneath the sun-drenched sky. The heat between us intensifies, our laughter mingling with whispers of longing. The water serves as a playful accomplice, its gentle caress heightening the electrifying connection we share.

Between breathless kisses and stolen glances, we tease and flirt, allowing desire to guide us towards new and exhilarating heights. The ocean becomes our sanctuary, a realm where passion and intimacy meld into one.

"You are something else, my Darling," he says. "You fit like a glove and meet my every need."

I wink, then lean over and breathe heavily in his ear. "Fuck me, Sean Irish."

He does, thrusting and pumping as the salty sea swishes around us. He reaches a hand under my top and tweaks my nipples in the most sensual way. He seems to know what my body will respond to—better than I know it myself. I become putty in his hands, enjoying every tiny movement.

He finishes first. I'm on birth control, so I don't worry about an accidental pregnancy. I think I know enough about him that I don't need to worry about

STDs either. He's a responsible guy. So I relax into it, feeling his warm liquid climb to the most dramatic heights inside of me. It feels incredibly good. Like a process completed that my body had yearned for.

I feel complete. I feel different. Evolved, maybe.

Alive. That's it. I feel alive, like never before.

We rock against each other, continuing the pleasure.

As a group of teenagers head our way with boogie boards in hand, we reluctantly part, our bodies still buzzing with the electric current of our connection. Our eyes meet, a shared understanding passing between us—a promise of more to come.

"Darling," Sean whispers, his voice filled with a mixture of awe and longing, "I can't put into words what you do to me. This is just the beginning of something extraordinary."

A wave of contentment washes over me, my heart swelling with affection. "This moment, this connection we share—it's everything I've ever hoped for. I think I'll keep you. If you'll let me."

CHAPTER 15

SEAN

By the time we arrive back at the airport to board our flight to Grand Cayman Island, Clara and I are holding hands and finishing each other's sentences like an old married couple.

Our bodies are still charged with the electric energy of our ocean encounter. We move in sync, exchanging knowing glances. The bond between us feels unbreakable, as if we've known each other for a lifetime.

This is it. The love of my life. What could possibly go wrong?

As we approach the boarding gate for our flight to Grand Cayman Island, anticipation fills the air. Clara checks her email, her eyes widening with a mixture of surprise and concern. Curiosity piques within me, and I lean in closer to read the message over her shoulder.

"What does it say?" I ask, my voice filled with curiosity.

She takes a deep breath, her expression a mix of disbelief and uncertainty. "Sean, the trip I won ... it was for engaged travel agents. The resort in Grand Cayman expects me to arrive with a fiancé. They just sent me a check-in form and there's a huge space at the top for my fiancé's name. What do I do? I never would have come on this trip if I'd known—"

I laugh and pinch her tush. "Well, you've already come on this trip, haven't you, Darling?"

"Indeed, I have," she replies, giving my shoulder a playful poke. "It was glorious."

A spark of mischievousness flickers in my eyes as a thought takes hold. "Well, then, it seems we have an opportunity to put our acting skills to the test. How about I pretend to be your fiancé?"

A huge smile spreads across her face. "Sean, are you serious? You'd be willing to go along with that charade?"

I squeeze her hand. "Absolutely, my Darling. Think about it. We'll get to experience paradise together, and it'll be an adventure filled with fun and spontaneity. We can be the happy, adventurous couple who captures everyone's attention."

Clara's eyes light up with a sexy glimmer, and she squeezes my hand in response. "You know what, Sean Irish? I think this could be a lot of fun. Let's do it. Let's give them the performance of a lifetime."

Every time she calls me Sean Irish, I feel like I'm back in that ocean, buried deeply inside of her. I hope the feeling never goes away. I hope to be a ninety year-old man someday, still going weak in the knees when she calls me Sean Irish.

With a shared understanding and a newfound excitement, we board the plane.

We find ourselves in separate rows, but I waste no time in striking up a conversation with the person sitting beside Clara. Through some friendly negotiation, I manage to trade seats, ensuring that I'm right beside my love for the duration of the flight.

Did I just refer to her as my love?

Yep. You betcha.

As the plane takes off, we settle in, the thrill of the upcoming charade still buzzing in the air. Clara checks her phone again. "Sean, I've been thinking. If we're going to play the part of an engaged couple, we should be flawless. We need to know everything about each other."

I nod, a smile of anticipation spreading across my face. "You're absolutely right. It's time for a serious talk. We'll have to dive deep into each other's lives, discover quirks and secrets, and create a narrative that no one can resist."

Our conversation becomes a whirlwind of questions and revelations. We delve into our pasts, sharing childhood stories and memorable experiences. We discuss our dreams and aspirations, uncovering common goals and shared desires.

As the plane soars through the sky, a sense of excitement fills the cabin. Clara and I laugh and whisper, finishing each other's sentences with ease. I can't be sure since I'm on the inside, but I'm fairly certain Clara and I now appear as two halves of a whole, perfectly in sync.

Her eyes meet mine, a mix of gratitude and admiration shining in her gaze. "I can't thank you enough for being willing to step into this role. I'm excited."

I squeeze her hand, my heart brimming with affection. "I'd do anything for you, my Darling."

The song I'm writing for Clara is beginning to form in my mind, and I absentmindedly sing a few bars.

> *Give me your worst*
> *I'll give you my best*
> *Let me get to you first*
> *You can forget all the rest*
> *United we'll stand*
> *We won't divide and won't fall*
> *Be my darling, my love,*
> *Let's climb right over these walls*

The tune is moody, with one note repeated frequently and dissonant tones that resolve into feel-good, harmonious chords. It hasn't fully developed in my mind yet, but I think it would work best as a country song. One of the hip, lively ones.

"Is that it?" she asks, her eyes wide.

"What?" I reply.

"Is that … my song?"

I break into a big smile. I can't help myself. She's excited, and I'm so glad. "Maybe."

Her smile turns into a frown as she swats at me. "You devil, you," she says through gritted teeth. "If that's my song, I want to hear it. Don't keep it from me. Please."

I sigh. "You'll hear it, when the time's right. I promise."

She rolls her eyes and folds her arms across her midsection. "Patience has never been one of my strong suits," she mutters.

Instead of saying more, I lean over and kiss her gently on the lips. Before I pull away, I hum another bit of the song. If looks could kill, I'd be a dead man right now.

"Oh, sorry," I say, teasingly. "What were we talking about? Patience. Yeah, that's it."

"Sean Irish, you are the devil," she says. "I swear!"

I enjoy this version of Clara. She's loosened up compared to the shy woman I met on day one of filming for the docu-series a couple of months ago. She seems way more comfortable in her own skin. The ease looks good on her. I'm happy to have helped work some of the kinks out.

As our plane begins its descent into Grand Cayman Island, ominous clouds loom on the horizon, signaling an approaching thunderstorm. The atmosphere inside the cabin grows tense, and the anticipation of the rough ride ahead weighs heavily on Clara's nerves. I can sense her anxiety, her jumpy reactions to every bit of turbulence that rocks the aircraft.

"Darling, it's going to be okay," I say, my voice soothing and steady. "I'm right here with you, and I promise you'll get through this."

She clings to my hand, her grip tight as we brace ourselves for the bumpy journey ahead. The roar of thunder echoes through the cabin, accompanied by flashes of lightning that illuminate the darkened sky outside.

The turbulence intensifies, and Clara's breath quickens. I turn to face her, my eyes filled with reassurance. "Remember, turbulence is normal. It might feel rough, but the plane is built to handle it. We're in good hands. We're *okay*."

She nods, her gaze seeking solace in mine. "I know, Sean. It's just ... it's only my second time flying, and it's a lot to take in. Reading about turbulence or watching on TV or a movie is one thing. Actually experiencing it is quite another. It's terrifying. It feels like we will fall right out of the sky."

I gently stroke her hand with my thumb, my touch meant to calm her racing heartbeat. "I understand, but we won't fall out of the sky. Aerodynamics don't work like that. It can be overwhelming, but I'm here for you. I promise."

"Have you flown a lot?" she asks.

"Oh, yeah," I say. "A ton. I've been on probably hundreds of flights, at this point."

"That's a lot of flying."

"It becomes no big deal, once you've done it a few times. Like riding in a car."

"I guess I can see that," she replies. "Although, I'm still scared right now. Those storm clouds look menacing."

"Hey," I say, giving her a wink and a smile. "Together, we'll ride out any storm, both figuratively and literally."

She chuckles.

"What?" I ask. "You think I'm a cheeseball, don't you?"

She lifts her fingers, keeping her index finger and thumb about an inch apart. "A tiny, little bit," she replies with a laugh. "But in a good way."

As the plane jostles through the turbulence, I keep my focus on Clara, offering words of encouragement and reassurance. We share stories, trying to distract ourselves from the unsettling experience. With each tale and every shared laugh, her tension eases, and a sense of calm settles over her.

Nearly an hour passes, and the storm eventually subsides, giving way to clear skies. The plane glides smoothly towards the landing strip, the once tumultuous ride now a distant memory.

As we step off the plane and onto the warm tarmac of Grand Cayman Island, Clara looks at me with gratitude shining in her eyes. "Thank you. I couldn't have gotten through that without you."

I wrap my arms around her, pulling her into a comforting embrace. "You're welcome, my Darling. I'll always be here to support you, no matter what challenges come our way. This trip is just the beginning of our grand adventure."

Her head rests against my chest, and I can feel her steady breaths as she regains her composure. The world around us fades into the background as we stand there, holding each other.

"We're really in paradise now," I say, my voice soft but filled with determination. "And this engaged couple is going to create unforgettable memories. Our engagement might be fake right now, but who knows what the future holds? Let's live it up. Yeah?"

She lifts her head, her eyes shining with excitement. "Absolutely, Sean. Let's live in the moment, embrace the unexpected, and create a love story that will surpass even our wildest dreams."

I nod. "Me and my Darling."

"Hey, wait," she says. "Aren't you supposed to be filming me for the docu-series? I'd almost forgotten."

"Yeah? So?"

"How is that going to work when we're playing fake fiancés? Won't Sonny be mad?" she asks.

"Sonny will be fine," I say. "We're adults, and we can do whatever we want. I'll figure a way to work it in. Don't you worry about it, okay?"

"Okay, fiancé, if you insist," she says sweetly.

"Oh, I'm going to insist on a lot of things while we're on this island," I tease as I kiss her more deeply. "Get used to it."

Hand in hand, we step forward, ready to embrace the adventures awaiting us on this beautiful island. As the evening sun casts its warm glow upon us, I can't help but feel an overwhelming sense of gratitude for the path that brought Clara into my life.

Together, we'll navigate the twists and turns of our pretend engagement, cherishing the connections we make, and perhaps discovering a love that's real and everlasting.

And … we'll have a ton of hot and steamy sex. Can't forget the sex.

CHAPTER 16

CLARA

As Sean and I step off the plane onto the sun-drenched grounds of Grand Cayman Island, a sense of excitement bubbles within me. The salty breeze carries the promise of adventure, and I can't help but feel a thrill running through my veins.

We make our way to the baggage claim and then the car rental counter, ready to embark on the next leg of our pretend engagement.

"Darling, my dear fiancé, shall we make our way to the resort in style?" Sean says, a silly grin on his face.

It's funny. We haven't talked about it, but from what Sean has said, I suspect he has a lot of money. Money he probably wouldn't mind spending on things that would create some extra fun.

I play along, raising an eyebrow. "Of course, my charming fiancé. We need to make a grand entrance, after all. What do you have in mind?"

He winks, then points to let the clerk know our

order. We're on the same page, our ease and connection still going.

"I thought you'd never ask, my Darling," he says as he pulls out a black AmEx credit card and completes the transaction. "It's time to splurge, don't you think?"

"Absolutely," I say. "Let the good times roll."

Moments later, with the car keys in hand, we make our way to the parking lot, where a sleek red convertible awaits. The tropical wind tousles our hair as we cruise along the scenic roads, laughter and banter filling the air.

We cruise through the streets of George Town, then all the way up to West Bay on the Western edge of the island before heading to our resort in Grand Harbour. The sun begins to set as we pull in. The sparkling blue sea shimmers nearby.

"Looks like we'll have a great view," I say. "This is amazing."

"Which part?" he asks.

"Every part," I reply.

He raises his brows. "I seem to remember you saying the word amazing at South Beach when we were … umm hmm … in the water. Maybe we can recreate that scene out here, at Seven Mile Beach?" He motions toward the water.

"I don't know," I say. "I'm not as wild and brave as I might appear. What happened at South Beach would shock my friends. It isn't exactly normal for me to have sex at a public beach."

He shrugs. "That's part of the fun, isn't it? And besides, no one saw anything. It isn't like we got freaky next to toddlers in the shallows. We kept our distance from other people. And please, Darling, call it making love. That was more than just sex."

"Yeah," I reply.

"Hey," he says, "I don't know about you, but today has been one of the best days of my entire life. I, frankly, don't care what anyone but you and me think about it. I intend to keep the attitude for the rest of our time here on the island. It's about you and me, Darling. Just the two of us."

To that, I smile much bigger. There's something about Sean's carefree vibe that brings me right out of my shell. It's almost like he's exactly what I need.

"A penny for your thoughts?" he asks.

"Oh, just thinking about how you open me up in ways I didn't know were possible. You make the world seem bigger and brighter. I've needed that. *So* much. You have no idea."

"Tell me, then," he says.

I shake my head. "Not now. I'm too tired. I want to get inside and lie down. It's been a long day."

After a few steamy kisses, we step out of the car, both of us wearing broad smiles. As we enter the lobby, I can't help but feel a mix of excitement and amusement. This entire trip, now filled with pretense and make-believe, is turning out to be more entertaining than I ever imagined.

The resort's reception desk is adorned with tropical flowers. A friendly receptionist greets us with a warm smile. "Welcome to Paradise Isle Resort. How may I assist you today?"

I step forward, glancing at Sean with a playful twinkle in my eyes. "We have a reservation under the name of Clara Darling and ... Sean Irish," I say, my voice laced with a hint of mischief. "I'm a travel agent from the United States. I entered a contest and won a free trip here."

The receptionist checks her computer, her eyebrows furrowing slightly. "I'm sorry, but our records show that this reservation is for an engaged couple. We'll need proof of your engagement."

"Seriously?" I ask. "Who asks for proof of engagement?"

She eyes us curiously, as if she can see through our charade. "Fine," she says. "Have you set a date for the wedding yet?"

I purse my lips, but Sean blurts, "Christmas! We thought it would be fun to get married at Christmas-time. You know, with a sleigh and eight tiny reindeer. Santa in his big red coat. The works."

Appearing even more skeptical now, the woman asks, "And where will this Christmas wedding take place?"

It's my turn, so I jump in. "We were considering hosting it here, at your resort. A destination wedding with about a hundred of our closest friends and family members in attendance," I say. "Can you accommodate a group that large?"

At this, the woman's eyes light up and dollar signs practically appear in front of them. "Oh, well, that would be lovely," she replies. "I'm not sure about the sleigh, unless we put it on water skis. We can find someone to dress up like Santa, though."

"That sounds nice," I reply.

"It's actually pretty here at Christmas," she continues. "The island gets all dolled up with holiday decorations and lights. There's a Christmas Market. You might be pleasantly surprised."

The woman glances at my hand, then makes eye contact with me briefly. She's suspicious.

Shit.

"Where's your engagement ring?" she asks.

I exchange a quick glance with Sean, and we both burst into laughter. It's a moment of hilarity, realizing the absurdity of our situation. But I quickly compose myself, pulling out a ring from my bag.

"Here's the proof you're looking for," I say, sliding the ring onto my finger. "Our love is so strong, we forgot to bring the ring with us. But worry not, it's all part of our whimsical adventure."

Sean chimes in, a mischievous grin on his face. "Yes, indeed. It seems our love is too spontaneous for convention. We're here to have the time of our lives, engaged or not."

He grabs me into a passionate embrace, then dips me low and kisses me deeply.

When we stand, the receptionist looks at us with a mixture of amusement and understanding. "I must say, you two are quite the charming couple. We'll make a note in our records. Enjoy your stay!"

As we make our way to our room, Sean and I burst into laughter once again, the absurdity of our fake engagement sinking in. It feels like we're characters in a romantic comedy, and the lines between pretense and reality blur with each passing moment.

"I guess we passed snuff once she heard we might bring a big crowd here for our destination wedding," I say with a laugh.

"Money talks," he replies. "But where'd you get that ring?"

"It's Ella's, actually," I explain. "She made me bring it and promise to wear it when I dress up for an evening out. Luckily, I remembered I had it when Desk Lady was grilling us. Proof of engagement ... who asks for that? Truly."

Inside our room, we collapse onto the plush bed, still giggling like school children. The tropical breeze flows through the open balcony, filling the room with the intoxicating scent of the sea.

"Clara, my fake fiancé, we sure know how to make a scene, don't we?" Sean says, his eyes sparkling with amusement.

I shake my head, a grin spreading across my face. "I never could have imagined that winning a trip would lead to all of this. But I have to say, I'm enjoying every moment of our little charade."

He leans closer, his voice low and husky. "Well, my pretend bride-to-be, let's make the most of this adventure. We'll dazzle everyone with our chemistry, leaving them guessing if our love is real."

As we settle down on the plush bed, our laughter subsiding, a sense of contentment fills the room. The tropical breeze caresses our skin, a gentle reminder of the paradise that awaits us outside.

We gaze into each other's eyes, the playful facade of our fake engagement giving way to a deeper connection.

"Darling," Sean says, his voice soft and filled with genuine affection, "this engagement may be a charade, but I can't deny the connection that has blossomed between us. I'm grateful for this opportunity to get to know you on a deeper level."

A warmth spreads through my chest, and I reach out to caress his cheek, my touch filled with tenderness. "It's funny how life works sometimes. Isn't it? Our paths crossed unexpectedly, and now we find ourselves embarking on an adventure that feels more real than anything I've ever known."

He leans in, his lips brushing against mine in a gentle kiss. "Clara, let's embrace this adventure fully. Let's make the most of our time here on Grand Cayman Island. What do you say we plan our activities for tomorrow?"

I smile and nod in agreement. "I love the sound of that, Sean. Being a travel agent, I already have a list of places I'd like to see."

"Let's do it," he replies. "You take the lead. I'll follow you anywhere you want to go."

I nod again, feeling like I can do a good job of planning for the both of us. "Tomorrow, let's explore the crystal-clear waters and vibrant marine life of Stingray City. And then, perhaps we can indulge in some relaxation at the beach, savoring the sun and sand."

Sean's eyes sparkle with excitement, mirroring my own enthusiasm. "Yes, Stingray City is nice. We can snorkel and let the wonders of the underwater world captivate us. Then, we can spend the afternoon lounging on the beach, enjoying each other's company. And maybe going for a little swim, if you know what I mean."

I blush. I know exactly what he means.

As we plan our day of adventures, the anticipation builds within us. Our hands intertwine. It's not just about the activities themselves. It's about the experience of creating memories together, of weaving a story that will forever be etched in our hearts.

As we lie there, gazing into each other's eyes, the boundaries of our pretend engagement blur further. It's as if the universe has conspired to bring us together, igniting a passion and connection that neither of us expected.

"Darling," Sean whispers, his voice husky with desire, "I want to explore more than just the island tomorrow. I want to explore the depths of our connection, to discover the nuances of your soul."

A surge of longing courses through me, and I move closer to him, our bodies molding together. "Sean, I feel the same way. Let's embrace every moment, every touch, and let our desires guide us. Tomorrow will be a day of adventure in more ways than one."

We lose ourselves in each other's embrace, the room filled with a symphony of whispered promises and passionate kisses. The lines between reality and pretense fade away, leaving only the raw connection that has blossomed between us.

As the night unfolds, the boundaries of our relationship continue to blur, and we surrender to the intoxicating dance of intimacy. In each other's arms, we find solace, passion, and a love that defies the constraints of time.

Our bodies entwined, our souls intertwined, we succumb to the magic of the moment, eagerly anticipating the adventures that await us on Grand Cayman Island, both above and below the surface of the crystal-clear waters.

Tomorrow will be a day of exploration, of discovering the wonders of the island, and of delving deeper into the depths of our love.

But Sean and I can't wait until tomorrow. We want each other tonight.

"You're so beautiful, Darling," he says as he gently lifts me and carries me out onto the balcony overlooking the beach.

"Are you going to stand out here naked and call my name?" I ask playfully. "Like you did at Rosie and Patrick's party last night?"

He laughs. "Yeah, maybe. Did my plan work? Did I get your attention?"

I kiss him, our tongues finding each other and dancing together like old pros. "You have my attention," I say.

"Good," he replies, pushing me gently against the railing and lifting my maxi dress. I'm still wearing my clothes from South Beach, swimsuit and all. "Then lean back and let me devour you."

I relax as his mouth explores my most sensitive

spots. The sensations send me to places I've only imagined.

"Oh, Sean," I mouth as I clutch his head, my eyes rolling back in mine.

CHAPTER 17

CLARA

Grand Cayman Island
Day 1

As the morning sunlight filters through the curtains, casting a golden glow across our suite, I find myself curled up next to Sean, our bodies intertwined. The rhythmic sound of the ocean waves serves as a gentle lullaby, soothing my senses and grounding me in the present moment.

I could get used to this. I hate to sound like a gold digger, but I'm pretty sure Sean could easily afford to buy us a condo or a little cottage down here, should I one day become his real-life fiancé.

Hmmm.

With a smile on my lips, I reach for my phone on the nightstand, eager to share the joy and excitement that has blossomed within me. I feel like a new woman. That timid, shy person who stepped on the plane at the Nashville airport bright and early yesterday morning seems long gone.

"Gotta call my girls," I mumble.

I dial the number of my best friends, Rosie and Ella, ready to divulge the unexpected turn of events in my life.

Well, I just call Rosie, actually, but she'll get Ella on the line soon enough.

The phone rings, and my heart beats faster with anticipation Rosie's voice fills the line, tinged with curiosity. "Clara! What's up? You sound unusually chipper."

I think I hear Patrick groan in the background. I must have woken him up.

I giggle, unable to contain my excitement. "You won't believe what happened, Rosie! Remember that trip I won? Well, it turns out it was for *engaged* travel agents, and so … I'm here with a fake fiancé."

"A what? You've got to be kidding. That sounds like something Ella would get herself into."

"Nope. Not kidding."

"Wait. Let me get Ella on the line," she says, then she puts me on hold.

There's a moment of silence on the other end, followed by an explosion of laughter. Rosie and Ella have completely lost all composure, their amused voices blending harmoniously in my ears.

"Clara, you're kidding, right?" Ella growls in her signature deep voice. "A fake fiancé? You always know how to make life interesting. Granted, though, that sounds like something I'd do."

Rosie chuckles. She was right. "Where'd you find him?" she asks.

I can practically picture their grinning faces, their eyes sparkling with amusement. "I'm serious, you two! It's all part of the adventure. His name is Sean, and it's been quite a whirlwind. We're playing the part, and let me tell you, it's turning into something more."

Rosie's voice takes on a tone of disbelief. "So, you're telling us you're falling for this guy, even though it's all pretend?"

I pause for a moment, my heart swelling with emotion. "It's hard to explain. Our connection is undeniable. Yesterday felt like a million hours and a million miles. So much happened. It opened up something unexpected and beautiful between us. There's a spark, a genuine affection that's growing with each passing moment. And besides, it's only the engagement that is pretend, and it didn't come up until we checked into the resort last night. For most of yesterday, we were just two lonesome travelers falling in love."

"Yeah, um, I was looking more closely at that picture you sent us from Miami," Rosie says. "You didn't tell us that Sean is *our* Sean, the camera guy. I knew he looked familiar, but it took me a little while to figure out why."

"I wasn't trying to hide anything from you," I say. "I've had my eye on him for a while. I was just too shy to say anything. We bumped into each other at your party, Rosie, and finally had a chance to chat. And then, well, he sat next to me on the plane."

"You mean randomly?" Rosie asks. "Or was that planned?"

"I thought it was random, at first," I say. "In fact, he was wearing a hat and sunglasses, so I didn't even realize it was him until we were all cozied up by each other."

"That sounds wild, Clara," Ella says. "I'm proud of you! I knew you had it in you."

"Yeah, thanks," I say. "But you know I've liked him. I'm pretty sure it was day one of filming for the docu-series when I said how the redheaded camera man was cute. That's my Sean."

"I remember!" Ella replies. "You did say that."

Ella's voice softens, her tone filled with warmth. "Clara, we want nothing but the best for you. If this is something real, something that fills your heart with joy, then we're behind you one hundred percent. We've been telling you to get your lady lace tickled by a set of strong hands. Sean's hands fit the bill"

I laugh. "Lady lace, huh? There it is. I was trying to come up with one of your strange names for genitalia yesterday, but couldn't do it. Glad you're here to fill in the gaps."

"It's kind of my job in our little group. Isn't it?" Ella asks. "I'm the wild, unabashed one. Someone has to be. You two are wound tighter than the antique clock on my grandma's mantle."

"Which is perfectly okay," Rosie says, jumping to our defense. "I found Patrick, and now it sounds like Clara has a new love of her own. I'd say we're doing alright.

You're the single one, Ella. Maybe we need to start poking at you."

"I brought a date to your engagement party," she says to Rosie.

Rosie laughs. "Yeah, was he even legal drinking age? I'll bet you had him dressed and shoved out the door before the sun came up the next morning."

"Okay, you've got me there," Ella replies. "My turn will come around … one day. Until then, I intend to have as much fun as humanly possible."

"Yeah, yeah," Rosie says. "This isn't about you, so I'll let the matter rest. Today, we're happy for our dearest Clara. It's her moment."

"Agreed! Woo-hoo, Clarebear!" Ella says enthusiastically. "You go, girl!"

Tears of gratitude fill my eyes as I lie there, listening to the unwavering support of my best friends. "Thank you, ladies. Your understanding and encouragement mean the world to me. This adventure, whether it leads to something more or not, has already brought me so much happiness."

The conversation continues, as we share stories and laughter, bridging the distance between us with the unbreakable bonds of friendship. Rosie and Ella promise to be there for me, offering guidance and a listening ear, even from afar.

"Hey, how are things at home?" I ask. "Does Matt seem to be holding down the fort for me? I tried to take care of all my existing clients before I left so he didn't have much to do."

"I think so," Rosie says, although I can't be sure. I

don't know enough about what you do to really tell with any degree of certainty. I could ask him, though."

"Want me to rough him up?" Ella asks playfully.

"No need for any of that," I say. "I'm sure it's fine. Everyone else okay?"

"Yep," Ella says.

"How about the new puppy, Rosie?" I ask. "How's little Penny?"

As if on cue, Penny whimpers in the background. Her little voice is so sweet. It makes me think about Caroline the sheepadoodle that I hope to adopt someday. "Aww," I say.

We hear Rosie and Patrick's muffled voices as they discuss who will take her out to pee. It's Patrick's turn, by the sound of it. They're staying at Rosie's condo right now since Patrick was in a rental. They're on the hunt for a house to buy before their wedding next spring.

Something about their entire happy situation gives me a pang of jealousy. I want those things, too—the engagement, the puppy, a house in Loveland. Or maybe a farm.

I sigh, deciding to immerse myself fully in this fake engagement as a way to try it on. No one knows us here on Grand Cayman Island. It's the perfect opportunity to see how Sean and i go together before we get back home to Loveland and real life.

"Sounds like someone has to go," Ella says.

"Yeah, I should probably get moving, anyway," Rosie says. "Rachael and I have another wedding out at Chestnut Hill Lodge next weekend and we need to prepare. The bride loves peonies, so a thousand or so of them are now on their way to my shop. We'd better be ready when they arrive. Those lovelies aren't going to arrange or deliver themselves."

"Okay," I say. "Kiss Penny for me. Have a good week!"

"And I'll see you at lunch, Rosie," Ella says. "Clara, get you some, girl. Live it up!"

"That's the plan," I say. "I'll send pictures."

As I hang up the phone, a renewed sense of determination washes over me. I have my best friends in my corner, cheering me on, and Sean by my side, ready to explore the uncharted territory of our connection. We have six glorious days to do whatever we want before it's time to travel home.

I turn to him, his eyes filled with curiosity. He's still groggy. "Who were you talking to? You seem happier than ever."

A smile tugs at the corners of my lips as I snuggle closer to him. "I was talking to Rosie and Ella. I wanted to share this journey with them, to let them in on the magic that's unfolding between us. They're thrilled for me. For *us*."

His expression softens, his fingers tracing gentle patterns on my arm. "I'm glad you have them. And I'm grateful to be a part of this adventure with you. We may be claiming a pretend engagement, but I have a feeling our very real love story is just beginning to unfold."

"I like that," I say simply. "I hope so."

We pour two cups of coffee and move to the balcony of our suite, a gentle ocean breeze ruffling our hair. We quickly and naturally engage in spirited conversation, discussing the day's plans, particularly our much-antici-pated trip to Stingray City.

"So, Darling, are you ready to face the majestic stingrays?" Sean asks, a mischievous twinkle in his eyes.

I laugh, playfully nudging him. "Oh, please, Sean. I'm fearless when it comes to sea creatures. It's you who I suspect might be squeamish."

He feigns offense, a mock look of indignation on his face. "Me? Squeamish? Never. I'll have you know that I've bravely faced off against some of the fiercest marine life out there."

I raise an eyebrow. "Is that so? Care to enlighten me about these grand adventures of yours, Mr. Irish?"

Sean leans closer. I think he likes it when I call him Sean Irish.

"Why, of course," he says. "There was the time I valiantly battled a rogue crab on a deserted beach. It was a fight to the death, Darling. A battle for the ages."

I burst into laughter, unable to contain the amuse-ment bubbling within me. "A crab, huh? You truly are a brave soul. Where was that? Because I'm thinking American crab might be less threatening than Caribbean crab. These local bad boys look huge, if the dinner portions are any indication."

He chuckles, his eyes dancing with mirth. "Well, someone has to protect you from the ferocious sea crea-tures. I'll be your knight in shining armor."

I playfully roll my eyes, a grin stretching across my face. "Oh, please, spare me the heroics. But I appreciate the sentiment. Let's make a deal, though. We'll face the stingrays together, and if I see you flinch even a little, I get to tease you mercilessly."

Sean leans back, his hands raised in surrender. "You drive a tough bargain. You know what happened to poor Steve Irwin, don't you? After years of facing crocs and all sorts of other dangerous creatures, it was a stingray barb to the heart that killed him. I follow his kids on Twitter. He is sorely missed."

"Well, that is terribly sad," I reply. "Kind of brings us crashing back down to reality, doesn't it?"

"Yeah."

We sit quietly for a few minutes, pondering. Finally, Sean speaks.

"Steve was a fun guy. I think he'd want us to have fun, too. He'd be okay with our laughter, Darling. I know he would. He'd probably even be okay with us enjoying the stingrays today."

I nod. "I'm sure you're right."

"So, mark my words, I will be the epitome of brav-ery," Sean says.

We both dissolve into laughter, the return to playful banter a testament to the ease and joy we've found in each other's company. The fear and doubt that once weighed heavy on my heart feel a million miles away, replaced by a lightheartedness that only love can bring.

We shower together, which turns into a steamy love-making session. That man knows how to make me wild with desire. Luckily, we can take our time and enjoy each other this week.

Once we're satiated and clean, we dress and make

our way to Stingray City, hand in hand. Ella's ring is in place, showing the world that I'm an engaged woman.

I can't help but feel a sense of anticipation building within me. Together, we'll conquer our fears, face the wonders of the ocean, and create memories that will forever be etched in our hearts.

Little do we know that our first day of vacation on Grand Cayman Island will be more than just a day of teasing and laughter. It will be a turning point—a day that will cement our connection and affirm the depth of our feelings.

But for now, as we head towards the boat that will take us on our underwater journey, we revel in the joy of the present moment, cherishing the bond that has blossomed amidst the teasing tides.

"Kiss me, fiancé," Sean says as we lean on the metal railing and watch the shore grow small in the distance.

CHAPTER 18

SEAN

Grand Cayman Island
Day 2

As the sun climbs in the sky, casting a radiant glow upon Grand Cayman Island, Clara and I find ourselves at a charming café in George Town. The scent of freshly brewed coffee mingles with the tantalizing aromas of sizzling bacon and golden pastries, igniting our senses and setting the stage for a decadent brunch.

We sit at a table adorned with crisp white linens, a gentle breeze ruffling our hair as we gaze out at the sparkling blue waters. The menu tantalizes our taste buds with a delectable array of options, each dish more tempting than the last.

I lean in, my voice low and playful. "Darling, I have a feeling this brunch is going to be a feast for both our stomachs and our senses. Shall we indulge in the flavors of paradise together?"

"Um, yes, absolutely," she replies, her eyes dancing with mischief. "And I think you could say the same for this whole trip. Couldn't you? I believe indulgence is the order of the week."

I love those mischievous eyes. And I love it when she talks about how much fun we're having together.

"I'm so in love with you, my Darling," I say. "I don't want anything to go wrong."

"You're sweet," she replies.

We haven't outright said that we love each other yet. I think we're close. I might tell her that I love her at some point today. It's been on the tip of my tongue.

Our laughter mingles with the melodic notes of the café, as we dive into a spread fit for royalty. Fluffy pancakes drenched in luscious maple syrup, eggs Benedict topped with velvety hollandaise sauce, and platters of tropical fruits bursting with vibrant colors—each bite is bursting with delicious flavors.

As we savor the succulent dishes, our conversation takes a playful turn, filled with teasing banter and laughter. It's becoming our usual. I can't complain about that. Being with Clara is effortless. Like breathing.

We continue our charade of an engaged couple, leaning into the roles we've adopted with a sense of ease.

Suddenly, an older couple at the adjacent table catches our attention. The woman, her eyes sparkling with curiosity, turns to Clara with a warm smile. "Oh, dear, I couldn't help but overhear your conversation. You two make such a lovely couple. May I ask, what will your new last name be?"

Clara's playful facade falters for a moment, a flicker of uncertainty crossing her eyes. The question catches her off guard, and the weight of the implications settles upon her.

She glances at me, a hint of unease in her expression. "Well, um, actually, I haven't really thought about changing my last name. I'm not a piece of property to be acquired, you know?"

The woman nods understandingly, her voice filled with wisdom. "Ah, my dear, it's a big decision, isn't it? But take your time. There's no rush to make such choices. Love doesn't hinge on a name but on the connection you share."

Clara's shoulders relax, a smile returning to her lips. "Thank you. You're right. Love is about so much more than a name. It's about the bond we've formed and the experiences we're sharing."

I eye Clara, and she's rattled. Seeing her like this makes me nervous.

As the couple bids us farewell, Clara turns to me, her eyes filled with a mix of relief and vulnerability. "Sean, this whole engagement charade is fun, but sometimes it feels like it's moving too fast. I need a moment to catch my breath."

"Hey," I say, "this engagement is pretend, remember?"

"Well, it just got pretty real," she replies. "I've never envisioned myself taking my husband's last name. I'm not saying there's anything wrong with that, but I'm not sure it's right for me. I'm not prepared to make that kind of decision."

I reach out and take her hand in mine, my touch gentle yet reassuring. "I get that. We'll take things at your pace. This adventure is meant to be enjoyed, not rushed."

There was a moment the day before when she appeared similarly rattled.

A young girl, probably four or five years old, randomly asked Clara if she was going to be a mommy. I have no idea what prompted the question, but for a moment, Clara's eyes went wide and wild. She looked like a horse ready to shed its saddle and run free.

I don't want her to feel like that around me. Or about me. Or because of me.

Her tension eases, replaced by a renewed sense of excitement. "Thank you, Sean. Your understanding means the world to me. Let's focus on the present and the amazing experiences we have planned for today." A twinkle dances in her eyes as she continues, "We still have the Queen Elizabeth Botanic Park, a fancy dinner, and a night snorkeling in the bioluminescent bay. Today might end up even better than yesterday, which is a hard act to follow."

I lean over and nuzzle her neck. "Will there be time for a little nap in there somewhere, if you know what I mean? Maybe a few stolen moments in the botanical gardens will do."

She raises her brows. "I'd love that. I can't get enough of you, Sean Irish."

"The feeling is mutual," I say.

I'm not sure what prompts me to bring it up here and now, but I suddenly want Clara to know my family.

I decide to begin with some family photos. That way, when she meets them in person, she'll know a little about who is who.

I pull my phone out of my pocket and flip through my family album.

"What are you looking at so intently?" she asks between bites of her eggs.

She uses the red and white checkered napkin to wipe sauce from her lips. The motion makes me want to kiss those lips, as if I haven't done so hundreds of times already. I want more. So, I take it. I kiss her as passionately as is appropriate in this cafe, then I lift the phone to show her the photo I've selected.

"It's my grandpa," I say. "Remember me telling you about him?"

"Of course," she replies. "He'll come to live on the farm with you in Loveland when it's ready, right?"

"That's right."

"He looks like a nice guy," she adds. "He has friendly eyes. Like yours."

I nod my agreement. "He certainly is a nice guy."

"Tell me about him," she says. "What's his name?"

I flip through some other photos of Grandpa, holding them up for her to see each time I land on a new one.

"Seamus O'Shea," I reply. "But I just call him Grandpa. You can, too."

"That feels a little presumptuous, doesn't it? For me to call him Grandpa?" she asks.

I shrug. "He'll love you just as much as I do," I say. "I

think calling him Grandpa is fine. That's what he'll be to you, if the two of us stay together."

This seems to catch her off guard. She leans back in her seat and places her fork gently on the table. Her mouth tips downward and she lets out a long, slow sigh.

"What?" I ask. "Am I freaking you out by showing you pictures?"

She shakes her head. "No, but you're freaking me out with all this staying together and loving me talk, as if this is a real relationship."

"Isn't it?"

She scoffs. "I don't know, Sean. What is this to you?"

I recoil, not wanting to distance myself from Clara, but I'm not sure what to say. I don't want to push and send her running, that's for sure.

"I do love you," I say, my voice soft. She looks hard at me, searching for certainty. I take her hand in mine and try again. "I know it's fast and unusual the way we came together, but I've never felt like this before, Darling. I love you. I'm *in love* with you. And yes, I want this to be a real relationship. To me, it already is. Hell, I'd marry you today, if you wanted to do it. Right here on Grand Cayman Island."

Too far. I felt it the second the words left my lips.

That was too much. I'm too much.

She sits silently, but I can tell that she's stunned. She's processing. Or maybe she needs space to process this. I should probably give that to her.

"Um, I need to run to the ladies' room," she says,

scooting out of her chair and disappearing down a hallway near the kitchen.

"Take your time," I call after her.

What even was that? I ask myself.

Shit.

I debate what to do next. Do I dig in and try even harder to woo her and convince her my love is real? Or do I ease off the gas and let her come to me?

I decide that I need a second opinion. I pick up my phone and place a call, holding it close against my ear until I hear his familiar voice on the other end of the line.

"Son?" he asks.

"Hey, Dad," I say. "What's up?"

I relax instantly.

"All good here in the great State of Texas," he says. "Mild weather for this time of year. Enough rain to avoid drought. Can't complain. Wait a minute. Let me get your mother on the line."

"Okay," I say, even though I might prefer to talk to just Dad right now.

Mom comes on, all good cheer and loving energy. She's the best. None of us would make it ten minutes in this big world without that woman holding us together.

"Hi, Seanie," she says sweetly. "How's my boy?"

I smile. "Good, Mom. I'm in the Caribbean right now. On Grand Cayman Island. I'm doing a little filming down here, and I'll be playing a gig on Thursday night. I'm enjoying myself."

"Sounds like fun," Mom says. "Will you be on television? Can we watch your gig?"

It isn't an unreasonable question. Sometimes, I am on TV and they can watch me play.

"Not this time. At least, I don't think so," I reply. "I'll ask around and let you know if I'm wrong."

"Okay," she replies.

I almost tell them about Clara. In fact, I open my mouth, but don't find my voice. Instead, I ask what I must. What I've been avoiding in the hopes that it will have been nothing more than a bad dream.

"How's Uncle Finn?"

I can practically hear Dad shake his head and steeple his fingers together. "Not good, Seanie. Not good at all."

My heart sinks. I've been sick over this ever since the accident last week. Uncle Finn was riding his motorcycle near his home on Sanibel Island when a truck pulled out and ran him clean over. The driver, apparently, didn't see him or his bike.

"Are you going there?" I ask.

"We were just talking about that," Dad replies. "I think your mother and I should make the trip. I'm his decision maker for healthcare, and by the looks of things, there are some hard choices coming up."

I nod, choking back tears. "You taking Grandpa, too?"

"Yes," Dad says. "If this is the end, he will want to be with his son. Any father would."

That hurts my heart even more. I ache for Grandpa as he faces losing a child. No father should have to go through that. Our children are supposed to outlive us. When they go first, it seems to be against the natural order of things.

"Okay," I reply. "Should I come? I can cancel the gig and be there as soon as you need me. It's not like I can function without thinking about Uncle Finn all the time. Buck Davenport would understand."

"Buck Davenport, the country singer?" Mom asks.

"Yeah. That's the one. He's a nice guy."

"Seanie," she says sternly. "Finn would want you to play the gig and pursue your dreams. We all want that for you. Stay where you are. Hopefully, he'll hang on long enough for you to get to him when you return to the States."

They're so good. I smile through tears. "Okay," I say.

As I look out at the sparkling Caribbean sea, a thought occurs to me.

Is this why I'm pushing things with Clara?

Uncle Finn never married or had kids, even though he wanted to. He always said there would be time. But now it looks like his time has run out. I don't want to find myself in that position. I don't want my life to end before I find and experience the love and happiness in store for me. I don't want to end up like my Uncle Finn.

As fast as she left, Clara returns to the table and sits in her seat. I wipe my eyes, not wanting her to see me this upset. I'm not sure what I'm feeling, let alone how to explain it.

"Mom and Dad," I say, "I've got to go. I'll call you later. Okay? Keep me posted."

They say goodbye and I hang up the phone.

"You okay?" Clara asks, taking a sip of her soda.

I nod. "Yep. You?"

She nods as well. We finish eating and leave the cafe.

We've had enough of the heavy emotions for now, so we keep our conversation light.

As planned, we tour the botanical gardens, eat a fancy dinner out, and snorkel in the bioluminescent bay.

We'll circle around to these matters later. In the meantime, we live in the moment, enjoying each other's company without expectations.

It's all we can do.

CHAPTER 19

CLARA

Grand Cayman Island
Day 3

"Wake up, my Darling," Sean whispers into my ear.

We're sprawled out across the bed in our suite. The doors to the patio are open, and birds are beginning to sing their cheerful morning song. The sound of the ocean outside has become such a comfort. I'm not sure how I'll sleep again without it's ancient rhythm lulling me into peaceful dreams.

"What time is it?" I ask as I stretch, then curl back into Sean.

We had a few uncomfortable moments yesterday at the cafe, but once we lightened the conversation, the day went beautifully. I hope this doesn't mean that we'll have trouble going deep when it's time. I don't want a shallow connection. I look forward to going deeper.

I suspect my own issues are at play, causing a bit of a

slow down as our relationship moves forward. I'll have to work on that. I've got plenty of time, right?

"I'm not sure what time it is," he says, kissing my neck. "But I have a special surprise planned. I'm excited to get started."

"Oh, you do, huh?" I ask, my voice still heavy with sleep. "What do you have in mind?"

As I roll closer to him, I feel his morning erection reaching out for me. He looks and feels so delicious. I reach down and take him into my hands. He tenses at my touch, then places his hand between my legs, his fingers encircling my lady lace, as Ella called it.

She is such a hoot.

"I think I should make sweet love to you before I tell you about my surprise," he says, his tone sultry. "Do you mind waiting a while longer?"

I don't hesitate. "Fuck me, Sean Irish," I say through gritted teeth.

I've learned by now that it makes him absolutely wild with desire when I say that. It's becoming our routine.

I love it.

He climbs on top of me, slowly moving his mouth down my body until he reaches my wet spot. He licks and chews in the most tantalizing way. I'm putty in this man's hands. I arch my back and curl my toes as he works his magic.

When he's done and I've come—*hard*—I roll over the side of the bed and invite him to enter me from behind. I'm learning that's his favorite position. I don't mind it myself.

"Wait," he says, gripping my hips.

His erection is throbbing with desire. I can feel it.

"Is something wrong?" I ask, hoping the answer is no. I might have come once already, but I plan to do it again.

"No, of course not," he says. "I was just thinking … ever since we got into this suite with the balcony, I've fantasized about bending you over it and fucking you out there in the open air."

"Sean Irish," I say, "you naughty boy. Someone might see us."

"So?" he asks. "What if they do? That's part of the thrill, isn't it? We're a happily engaged couple, remember?"

My … lady lace … is aching for more of him. The thought of being out there in the warm, morning air does sound pretty nice. Plus, it will be a memory we won't forget.

"Okay," I say. "Let's do it. Fuck me on the balcony, Sean Irish."

He turns me, then lifts me into his arms, carrying me out onto the balcony. We're both completely naked—we slept that way—and the salty breeze feels delightful against my skin.

I lean over the balcony, taking a quick glance around to see if anyone is watching. There are a few people in the ocean, but they don't seem to be paying any attention.

I raise my naked backside up in the air, inviting Sean in.

"You are the most spectacular creature I've ever

seen," he says as he bends down and takes one long lick between my legs. "I'm the luckiest man alive."

Slowly, he pulls me toward him and slides inside. He moves gently at first, rocking me with the rhythm of the waves. As the sensations intensify, he moves faster ... and faster ... and faster. His throbbing cock pounds me in the most spectacular way. My body grips and pulls him in, further and further.

I glance over my shoulder at him, and I swear he looks like the king of the jungle right now. Some primal urge in him is being satisfied. I'm honored to be his chosen queen.

He rocks and pounds until we both come, together, gripping and wailing, trying to keep quiet so as not to disturb the peace.

"Thank you, my Darling," he says as he lifts me and carries me back to the bed. "That was something special."

I smile, completely satisfied. I haven't had this much sex before, but I'm finding it good for my body and soul. I feel loved and cared for in a way I didn't know was possible.

"Thank *you*, Mr. Irish," I say. "You're mighty good at that."

He raises his brows and makes a little fake salute motion that I find adorable. I genuinely like this guy.

"You're quite an inspiration," he says. "I'm glad I can make you happy."

We bask in the afterglow for a few minutes before either of us speaks. Finally, we're ready to start the day with more island adventures.

"Okay, spill it," I say.

He laughs. "Oh, I already did. Didn't you feel it? Want me to do it again, to review?"

We both laugh as I swat him on the shoulder. "Silly," I say.

"You want me to tell you about the surprise, huh?"

"Yes," I say. "What are you up to?"

"About 6'3" tall, last time I checked," he jokes. "I can do this all day."

"Seriously," I say, "tell me what you have planned."

"Fine," he says. "I've arranged for a day of pampering at the island's finest spa. You deserve some relaxation and time to yourself."

I feel a mixture of gratitude and apprehension, appreciating his efforts to give me a break but still grappling with the whirlwind nature of our relationship. "Thank you. I appreciate the gesture. A day at the spa sounds lovely."

He nods, his eyes filled with warmth. "You deserve to be treated like royalty. Take this day to unwind, reflect, and rejuvenate. And don't worry, I've got something special planned for later. Well, tomorrow night at the Buck Davenport concert, to be exact. It'll be a huge surprise."

"Should I be worried?" I ask. "I'm not usually a fan of surprises. I guess I like to be in control. I don't know."

"What's to worry about?" he asks.

I shrug. "Will I be embarrassed?"

"I don't think so," he replies. "You'll be with me. I hope you'll be happy."

I smile, genuinely touched by his thoughtfulness.

"That sounds wonderful, Sean. I'll make the most of this day and look forward to the surprise tomorrow."

I suspect it has something to do with the song he's writing for me, but I don't know for sure.

We part ways for the day, with Sean guiding me to the spa and ensuring I'm in good hands. As I step into the tranquil oasis, the scent of essential oils fills the air, instantly calming my racing thoughts. I surrender myself to the nurturing hands of the spa professionals, ready to embrace the serenity that awaits me.

Hours pass by in a blissful haze, as I indulge in relaxing massages, soothing facials, and the healing power of the spa's luxurious amenities. With each moment, the weight on my shoulders lightens, and I begin to find solace in the quiet sanctuary.

As the afternoon draws to a close, I make my way to the spa desk to check out. The attendant, a friendly woman with a warm smile, looks up from her computer screen. "Good afternoon, Mrs. O'Shea. I hope you enjoyed your day at the spa."

Confusion sweeps over me, and I stammer, "I'm sorry, but I think there's been a mistake. I'm not married."

The attendant's eyes widen slightly, her cheeks flushing with embarrassment. "Oh, my apologies, dear. I must have assumed when I saw your last name as O'Shea. Please forgive me."

I feel a mix of emotions rising within me—surprise, discomfort, and a touch of unease. It's a stark reminder of how fast things have progressed between Sean and me, how our fake engagement has inadvertently blurred the lines between our pretend and real lives.

With a composed smile, I reassure the attendant. "No worries at all. It's just a misunderstanding. Thank you for your help."

As I step outside the spa, the cool breeze caresses my skin, offering a moment of clarity. The encounter at the desk serves as a gentle reminder that I need to address my concerns about the pace of our relationship, to ensure that our foundation is built on solid ground.

With renewed determination, I make my way back to our suite, ready to have an open and honest conversation with Sean about my reservations and the need for us to take a step back and reassess our journey together.

As the door swings open, I find Sean waiting with a playful grin on his face. "Well, Darling, did you enjoy your day of relaxation?"

I take a deep breath, meeting his gaze with a mix of appreciation and determination. "Yes, Sean, I did. It gave me some much-needed time to reflect. But now, I think it's important for us to have a conversation."

His playful expression softens, replaced by a look of concern. "Of course, Clara. I'm here to listen. But first, your mom called."

"My who? Did what?"

"Your mom, Meghan Darling. She rang the landline here in the suite. I talked to her for a few minutes. Nice lady."

My heart races. Meghan Darling might sound like a

nice lady, but it's far more complicated. She didn't know about Sean. She probably won't react well.

Oh, no.

"She said for you to call her mobile when you get back."

I nod, then step inside and lean against the closed door.

Real life is coming for me, fast. I can't live in this bubble forever.

CHAPTER 20

SEAN

Grand Cayman Island
Day 4

"*R*osalie's Flowers, Rachael speaking."

"Hey, Racheal," I say, the phone clutched tightly in my hand. "This is Sean O'Shea. I'm one of the camera guys working with Sonny on the docu-series."

"You mean the naked guy on the balcony?"

I chuckle, not only because I made an impression at Rosie and Patrick's engagement party, but also because I was naked on a balcony less than an hour ago.

"Yep, one and the same," I say with a laugh. "Is Rosalie there?"

"Sure," Rachael replies. "Hold on."

I hear muffled talking in the background, then Rosie's voice on the other end of the line.

"This is Rosalie. How can I help you?"

I'm not sure I should call her Rosie, even though that's how I think of her since Clara always uses the nickname. "Hey Rosalie, it's Sean … O'Shea. I'm here on Grand Cayman Island with Clara. I mean, she isn't here with me right now. I'm trying to put together a surprise for her, and I'm hoping you can help."

"Sean, hi," she says, her voice tinged with curiosity. "I hear you and our Clara are having a lovely time together. How's everything going in paradise?"

"We sure are," I say. "It's a match made in heaven, if I do say so myself. We're definitely enjoying paradise."

Rosie giggles, and I get the idea she has me on speaker. Rachael is probably listening, too. I'm okay with that.

I pause for a moment, gathering my thoughts. "So, you remember your friend Clara, right?"

A hint of amusement enters her voice. "Of course, I do. The woman who unwittingly became engaged to you, right?"

I chuckle, feeling a weight lifted off my shoulders. "That's the one. Well, here's the thing. I'm planning a big surprise for her, something that I hope will show her just how much she means to me. And I was wondering … would you and Ella be able to fly down here to Grand Cayman?"

There's a moment of silence on the other end, as if Rosalie is processing the request. I realize that it's a big one. Then, her voice comes through, filled with genuine enthusiasm. "Sean, that sounds amazing! We'd love to be a part of it. Just give us the details, and we'll make it happen."

Relief washes over me, and I can't help but feel grateful for the unwavering support of Clara's best friends. "Thank you, Rosalie. I really appreciate it. I'll cover all the expenses, so you don't have to worry about anything. I just think it would mean the world to Clara to have you both here when I do the big reveal."

Rosalie's voice softens, filled with a mix of understanding and affection. "Sean, it's clear how much you care about Clara. We're happy for you both. We'll be there, no doubt about it. Just let us know the dates and any other information we need."

I wince as I tell her the date. "Can you be here tomorrow? The surprise is scheduled for tomorrow evening, at the Buck Davenport concert."

"Tomorrow?" she asks. "Like, as in the day after this one?"

"Yeah. Too soon?"

"When would we fly?" she asks.

"I don't know," I say. "Maybe tomorrow morning? I can check flights and call you back. Will Ella be okay with it, or should I call her, too?"

Rosie chuckles. "Ella is always up for something that has the potential to involve partying and casual sex. And an island setting makes those things even better. She's in. Don't worry about that for a minute."

"Good."

"But you couldn't possibly think I'd let you off the hook without telling me what this big surprise is, right?" she asks.

I laugh, knowing that Rosalie won't let me get away with keeping secrets. "Okay, I'll give you a few hints, but you have to promise not to spill the beans to Clara. It's going to be a night she won't forget."

Her voice takes on a playful tone. "I promise I won't ruin the surprise. Now spill the details!"

I take a moment, savoring the anticipation before sharing. "Alright, here's what I have planned. Tomorrow night, before my gig at the Buck Davenport concert, I'm taking Clara to a secluded spot on the beach. We'll have a private candlelit dinner under the stars, with waves gently crashing in the background. It'll be a moment of magic and romance."

There's a pause on the other end, followed by a gasp of excitement. "Sean, that sounds absolutely incredible. Somehow, I don't think you need Ella and me for dinner on the beach, though. What else is happening?"

She's quick.

"After dinner, when I open for Buck, I'll perform an original song that I've written for Clara, with Buck on backups."

"You're a songwriter? And a singer? I had no idea."

"I am," I say. "I've been writing songs for other artists for a long time now, but I'm finally ready to make a name for myself as a frontman. Clara actually gave me my stage name—Sean Irish."

"Aww," Rosalie replies. "How nice. You two are the cutest. I take it you are Irish?"

"Indeed."

I can't help but feel a surge of happiness hearing Rosalie's enthusiastic response.

"Thanks, Rosalie," I continue. "I want this night to be unforgettable for Clara. And having you and Ella there will make it even more special. Can you come down to the island to be with us?"

She's quiet for a moment, and I think I hear a pencil tapping in the background. "Hold on," she says. "Let me double check with Rachael. We have a wedding at Chestnut Hill Lodge on Saturday. Luckily, we have a summer intern helping out right now. Let me ask if they can handle things without me." She's gone for a few more minutes, then returns with good news. "I can do it! Ella and I will be there. Maybe Patrick, too. I'll call him to see what he has going on. Do you mind me bringing a plus one?"

"Of course not," I say. "You and Patrick are a package deal, as far as I'm concerned. I know Clara feels the same way. As long as someone can take care of Penny."

"I'll bet Brandon can," Rosalie replies. "I'll miss the baby dog, but she'll be fine for a few days without us. She's comfortable with Brandon."

"Good," I say. "Things are coming together, then."

Rosalie's voice softens, filled with warmth. "We're honored to be a part of this, Sean. Clara is lucky to have you. Just make sure to take a deep breath and enjoy the moment too. It's a milestone in your relationship, and you deserve to savor every second."

Her words sink in, reminding me of the importance of being present in this journey with Clara. "You're right, Rosalie. I'll make sure to soak it all in. And I can't wait for you both to be here and witness the magic firsthand."

"I can't wait either," she says. "Hey, did you know that Clara sings?"

"I didn't!" I say. "I mean, she sang beautifully with me at your party, but does she have more than party singing experience?"

"Oh, yeah," Rosalie says. "Our girl was a vocal performance minor in college. She would have made a career out of it, if she thought she could have earned a living that way. She has a set of pipes on her that you wouldn't believe."

"Wow," I say. "I had no idea. I love that we have a love for music in common. I'll be sure to ask her about that."

"Just don't tell her you heard it from me," Rosalie says. "Otherwise, she'll know we've been talking and will start playing detective."

"Right," I reply.

As we exchange a few more words, excitement continues to build within me. Having Rosalie. Patrick, and Ella there will not only provide support but also create a sense of unity and celebration. Our love story is evolving, and with their presence, it's bound to become even more extraordinary.

"Hey, Rosalie," I say, acting on a whim. I shove a hand through my hair nervously.

"Yeah, Sean?"

"Do you think Clara's parents would come down, too, if I invited them?"

I hold my breath as I wait for her response.

"Wow," she says simply.

"Wow, yes? Or wow, no?" I ask.

"I don't know, Sean," she says. "They aren't big travelers. And Meghan, Clara's mom, isn't always the most positive person. Sometimes, she can be a real downer."

"Clara is close to them, though, right? She talks about them."

I practically hear Rosalie shrug and nod. "Yeah, true. I don't know. I guess it can't hurt to ask. I can give you their number."

"Really?" I ask. "That would be amazing. I'd like to invite them. The worst they can say is no."

"Okay," she says. "I'll text you. Good luck."

I have more plans that I don't share with Rosalie. I don't intend to share all of the details with anyone except maybe Buck Davenport, since it's his show. Everyone else can be surprised along with my Darling. I hope she likes it.

With renewed excitement, I end the call, thanking Rosalie and promising to send all of the travel info.

I have a lot to do between now and tomorrow evening. If I want to pull this thing off, I had better get busy.

As I gaze out at the beautiful waters of Grand Cayman Island, I can't help but feel grateful for everything that has happened over the past few days. It hasn't even been a week since Clara and I first talked at Rosie and Patrick's engagement party, and look at us now.

The connections we've formed, the friendships that have blossomed, and the love that continues to grow is remarkable, if I do say so myself.

With the anticipation mounting, I look forward to the night that awaits us tomorrow—the night where love, music, and the serenity of the beach will converge, creating a moment that Clara will carry in her heart forever.

Now, I just have to keep my Darling occupied while I finalize the arrangements.

It's nearly lunchtime and she's spent the morning reading a romance novel on the beach. I decide we had better go and grab some food before I disappear to make preparations. We shower together, then pile in the car and head to George Town to try another waterfront restaurant.

I'm still getting used to driving on the wrong side of the road here, but I manage to get us to lunch safely.

A surge of gratitude swells within me, and I can't help but feel a renewed sense of purpose.

This is going to be so good. I can hardly wait!

My Darling has quickly become such a light in my life. I enjoy making her happy. I could spend the rest of my life doing just that.

CHAPTER 21

CLARA

Grand Cayman Island
Day 5

*I*t's our fifth day on Grand Cayman Island, and the pace has slowed.

Thank goodness!

At first, it was fun to race from one tourist attraction to another, but I'm tired. Today, I'm happy to lay on the beach all day under an umbrella as the gulls call and the waves crash nearby. Yesterday was a lazy beach day as well, and I didn't mind. Sean has been busy rehearsing for his gig that happens tonight. I'm looking forward to seeing him on stage, but I'm also enjoying the downtime while he's otherwise occupied.

I think my adrenaline was pumping so hard that first day on the plane and then in Miami. I needed time to recover and find a balance.

Now that I think about it, Sean and I need to find a balance. He's amazing, and I'm so happy to be with him. He's a lot, though. The whole thing is a lot. I'm so far outside of my comfort zone that I barely recognize myself. I look forward to getting back to Loveland and settling into a slower dating pace. I think it will be healthy to get to know Sean in a more normal setting, where we aren't faking an engagement.

For today, my only plans are to relax until it's time to get dressed for dinner and the concert. I already have a dress picked out. Sean bought it for me yesterday at one of the shops in George Town. It's a slinky, off-the-shoulder red number. I almost didn't let him buy it, but he convinced me that he'd enjoy seeing me in it. He might have mentioned taking me out of it after the concert, too.

Yum.

I pick up my phone to call Rosie and Ella. I forgot to tell Ella that I've been using her ring as a fake engagement ring. I know she won't mind, and I could certainly text to say so, but I'd like to hear their voices anyway.

I dial Rosie first, as usual. She doesn't pick up for several rings. When she does, there's all kinds of commotion in the background.

"Rosie?" I ask. "Where are you? It sounds like you're in the middle of a circus," I exclaim, trying to make sense of the background commotion.

Rosie chuckles, attempting to lower her voice amidst the noise. "Oh, you know us, Clara. Always on the go! We're running errands, but don't worry, we're looking forward to Sean's concert tonight. It's going to be amazing! You're going to put us on Facetime so we can watch along with you, right?"

I'd told them about the concert, and they'd made me promise to share some of it via Facetime. Assuming the cell signal isn't overloaded with so many people in one place, I should be able to make that happen.

A mischievous spark ignites within me, and I can't help but press for more information. "Errands? In such a lively place? Come on, give me a hint. I'm dying of curiosity."

Ella joins in the conversation, her laughter infectious. "Clara, you know we can't spoil the surprise. Just trust us, it'll be worth the anticipation. Enjoy the concert, and all will be revealed in due time."

My curiosity piqued, I playfully protest. "What surprise? No one told me anything about a surprise."

"You'll see," Rosie replies.

"You two are experts at teasing!" I say. "But I suppose I'll have to wait. Just remember, revenge is a dish best served cold."

Laughter rings through the phone, and the connection ends with a promise of an unforgettable surprise … somewhere, sometime. As I hang up, a mix of excitement and curiosity fills me. Whatever surprise awaits, I'm grateful to have friends who share in the joy of anticipation.

Then it hits me.

They might be talking about Sean's surprise that's supposedly happening at the concert tonight. Could it really be one and the same? Rosie and Ella couldn't be involved in that? Could they?

With a smile still on my face, I decide to call my mom and share the exciting news about Sean and the concert. I haven't returned her call from the other day, anyway, and I know she's probably been waiting.

As I dial her number, I hope to catch her in a more peaceful environment.

The phone rings a few times before my mom answers, her voice slightly muffled. "Hello, hun! Apologies for the background noise. I'm at the airport, and it's quite chaotic. But guess what? I have a surprise for you."

A sense of wonder washes over me as I realize the unexpected twist. "Mom, you're where? Is Dad with you, too?"

She chuckles, her voice filled with excitement. "Yes, dear! You'll know soon enough. Toodaloo!"

Amazement fills me as I respond. "Toodaloo?"

Who is this woman and what has she done with my mother? I just hope she's in a good mood. She seems like she is, so I'm hopeful.

As I hang up, a sense of joy and anticipation fills me. The pieces of the puzzle are aligning.

Might my friends and my parents be coming here, to Grand Cayman Island? I'd love that, if my mom can behave. I'd love for my parents to meet Sean, and I'd love for them and my friends to enjoy the island with us.

As I stand on the sandy beach, a gentle breeze caresses my face, carrying with it a sense of anticipation. Thoughts of a fun get-together on the island swirl in my mind, creating a wave of curiosity that I can no longer contain. My fingers tremble slightly as I dial

Sean's number, hoping he has some insight into the mysterious events unfolding.

Of course, he does.

The phone rings, and my heart quickens with each passing second. Just as I'm about to give up, a voice answers on the other end.

"Hello?"

"Hey, Sean. I hope rehearsals are going well," I say, attempting to keep my voice casual, masking the eagerness bubbling within me.

Who am I kidding? I sound nervous. I know, I do.

There's a brief pause before he responds, his voice filled with warmth. "Actually, Clara, I'm not at rehearsals right now. I'm ... out running errands."

Curiosity piques within me, sensing there's more to his statement. "Errands? What kind of errands?"

Sean hesitates for a moment, and in the background, I hear muffled voices, snippets of conversation that catch my attention. "Oh, just some last-minute things I needed to take care of. Nothing too exciting."

My ears perk up at the mention of an intriguing location. "Wait, is that ... a jewelry store I hear in the background?"

There's a brief silence, followed by a chuckle. "Caught me, huh? Yeah, I may or may not be at a jewelry store at the moment."

My heart skips a beat, and a smile tugs at the corners of my lips. Could he be shopping for something related to the surprise he has planned for me? The thought ignites a spark of excitement.

"Sean Irish, you sly fox. Is this jewelry store related

to the surprise you have planned for me tonight?" I ask, trying to contain the bubbling curiosity in my voice.

He laughs, the warmth of his laughter resonating through the phone. "Well, Darling, that's for me to know and for you to find out. But I promise, it's going to be worth the wait."

A mixture of anticipation and wonder courses through my veins. Whatever Sean has planned, it's clear he has put thought and care into every detail. With the knowledge that my loved ones are possibly on the island and the mention of a jewelry store, I can't help but let my imagination wander.

Would he actually propose to me? For real?

That's crazy thinking, right? We barely know each other. And the fake engagement is only that.

I take it a step further, though.

Would I want him to propose to me? Would I say yes?

As I hang up the phone, a sense of excitement lingers in the air. I find myself eagerly anticipating the surprises that await me. I set off for a walk along the beach, allowing the soft sand to carry my hopes and dreams, as I eagerly await the unfolding of this enchanting love story.

But I don't walk long before I dial Rosie and Ella again. I can't help myself.

What? Am I supposed to sit quietly and act like nothing is happening?

I can't do that. No way, no how.

I dial Rosie's number once again, eager to share the exciting revelation about Sean's whereabouts. The phone rings, and I can barely contain my excitement as my friends' voices fill the line.

"Hey. You won't believe it, but Sean is actually at a jewelry store right now," I say, my voice tinged with wonder and excitement.

Their gasps of—fake?—surprise echo through the phone, and I can sense their own curiosity growing. "A jewelry store? That's quite intriguing, Clara. It seems like Sean has something very special planned, if you get my drift," Ella responds, her voice filled with excitement.

Oh, I get her drift, alright.

A sense of awe envelops me as I continue, sharing the thoughts swirling in my mind. "You know, guys, I can't help but wonder ... What if Sean were to propose to me? Should I say yes? It's all moving so fast, but I can't deny the feelings that have grown between us. We fit together like two parts of one whole. And I don't just mean sexually."

Silence falls on the other end of the line, as if Rosie and Ella are taking in my words, their thoughts aligning with mine. Finally, Rosie's voice fills the void, her tone gentle yet filled with unwavering support.

"Clara, dear, only you can answer those questions. But remember, love has a way of guiding us to unexpected places. Trust your heart and embrace the journey," she says.

Her words resonate deep within me. She is a woman who practices what she preaches. She had to become open to love with Patrick, even though he was the last person she thought she'd end up with. Now she's deliriously happy, and I want the same happiness for myself.

Have I found true love with Sean?

Ella's voice joins the conversation, her excitement palpable. "And who knows what the future holds, Clara? This surprise Sean has planned might be the turning point, a milestone in your love story. Trust in the magic of the moment."

A shiver of anticipation courses through me, and I can't help but smile at the thought of what awaits. Before I can respond, Rosie interjects with a mischievous tone. "Oh, by the way, Clara, you might want to look behind you."

"What?"

Confusion fills me for a moment, but I turn around nonetheless, only to find myself frozen in disbelief. There, standing on the beach, are Rosie, Patrick, and Ella, wearing ear-to-ear grins. Time seems to stand still as we rush into each other's arms, a mixture of laughter and tears filling the air.

"How? What?" I ask as I hug them.

"Sean arranged everything," Rosie replies. "You can thank him."

Tears fill my eyes. I don't even know why. I'm happy, not sad.

I can't help but be overwhelmed by the love and support that surrounds me, and the feeling of being reunited with my dearest friends. In that moment, worries and uncertainties melt away, replaced by an unbreakable bond.

"Ladies," I ask my friends, "am I getting engaged tonight?"

"You tell us," Ella instructs. "But it sure seems that way."

Patrick chuckles. "Speaking as the only guy here … Yeah, um, I have to agree. Seems like Sean is going all out. I think he's a man who has fallen head over heels in love." He grabs Rosie and kisses her. "Believe me. It takes one to know one."

I smile, raising one shoulder like a blushing schoolgirl. This whole relationship is beyond my wildest dreams. It's perfect. For me, anyway. Like Cinderella and her slipper or Goldilocks and the things that were just right, I've found my perfect fit. And now, he's about to ask me to spend the rest of my life with him.

How did I get so lucky?

As we continue to embrace and celebrate on the sandy shores, I am reminded of the power of friendship, the strength it brings in times of joy and uncertainty. With Rosalie, Patrick, and Ella by my side, I feel invincible, ready to face whatever surprises lie ahead.

CHAPTER 22

CLARA

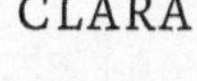

**Grand Cayman Island
Day 5**

The Evening of the Concert

Rosie, Ella, and I gather in the suite, buzzing with anticipation for the evening's concert. The room is a flurry of activity as we each prepare, selecting our outfits, carefully styling our hair, and applying the finishing touches of makeup.

As I slip into the vibrant dress that Sean picked out for me, a knock interrupts the flurry of excitement. I assume it's Sean at the door, ready to embark on this enchanting night together. I rush to open it, only to be greeted by a familiar sight that catches me off guard.

"Mom, Dad! What are you doing here?" I exclaim, a mixture of surprise and curiosity coursing through me.

Even though I suspected they'd be joining us, I wasn't sure. And besides, it's one thing to think about them showing up and quite another to see them on my doorstep, in the flesh. Not to mention, they don't travel much. How else do you think I made it to my late-twenties without having been on a plane?

My mom steps forward, her expression guarded. She's wearing a billowy dress and a straw hat with a wide brim. She looks the part of a harried tourist, her curly blonde hair tightening in the humidity. So does Dad. He's wearing a pastel pink button-down shirt with palm tree print and cargo shorts. The tropical print dances against his brown skin. Both of my parents are in sandals, which is an unusual sight.

They've put effort into this.

"Clara, we decided to surprise you," Mom says. "I've been told it's a big night, after all. We thought we'd support you. That's why we schlepped all this way in the summer heat. You know how the heat makes me irritable."

Her words are tinged with a hint of snippiness, and I can feel my defenses rising. It's no secret that my mom has a tendency to be critical, but tonight, I had hoped for positive vibes only.

Before tensions escalate, Ella steps in, her voice filled with calm authority. "Now, Meghan, let's not spoil this special night for Clara. We're all here to enjoy the concert and support her. Let's focus on that, shall we?"

There's a pause, a flicker of realization in my mom's eyes, and she nods, her features softening. "You're right, Ella. I apologize, Clara. I'm here to support you tonight, no matter what. You're our girl. We want you to be happy."

Mom reaches out to hug me, and her sentiment seems genuine. Dad winks as he looks on, approvingly.

Okay, then.

A wave of relief washes over me as my mom's apology sinks in. Perhaps tonight can be a turning point, a chance for us to set aside our differences and create new memories.

Perhaps I'm getting way, way ahead of myself, but a girl can dream, can't she?

As I start to respond, my phone buzzes, indicating a new message. I quickly check it, and a smile dances across my lips. It's a text from Sean, informing me that he'll meet me for dinner on the beach and has arranged for a driver to pick me up.

I relay the message to the others. "Sean will see me at our special dinner, and he's sending a driver. You all go ahead to the concert, and we'll catch up to each other later. Can you find something to eat on your own?"

Rosie and Ella exchange knowing glances. "I'm sure we can handle that," Rosie says.

"Sounds like a plan, Clara," Ella adds. "We'll make sure to save you a spot. Enjoy your time with Sean, and we'll meet you there."

Patrick and my parents nod their agreement as well.

"Go," Dad says. "We've got this."

With a sense of anticipation lingering in the air, I bid farewell to my friends and my parents, eager to reunite with Sean and embark on the next chapter of our adventure.

As I step into the awaiting car, I know that tonight holds the potential for unexpected surprises, laughter, and a deeper connection with the man who has stolen my heart.

I suspect it will be a night I'll never forget.

"Sean Irish, do your thing," I mumble to myself. "Sweep me off my feet. Oh, and become a country music star, while you're at it."

No pressure.

When I arrive at the secluded stretch of beach near the concert venue, a young man is holding up a sign with my name on it, like the kind you'd expect to see at the airport. Not that I've been to many airports, because … you know. But I've seen the signs on TV and in the movies. My name is written in neat block letters: Clara Darling.

With a warm smile, the messenger guides me through a path illuminated by soft, flickering candlelight.

The air carries a subtle hint of salt and the soothing melody of crashing waves. As we walk further, the sight that unfolds before me takes my breath away. A secluded spot, adorned with a tapestry of flickering candles, dances in the twilight. Delicate flowers, their vibrant colors reflecting the hues of the setting sun, grace the table and surround the intimate seating area.

The gentle rustling of palm trees adds a whisper of serenity to the ambiance. Soft strands of fairy lights twinkle above, casting a warm, ethereal glow. The gentle sea breeze carries the scent of blooming flowers, intertwining with the mesmerizing aroma of an exquisite meal being prepared nearby.

I take a seat, feeling a mixture of awe and anticipation coursing through my veins. The flickering candlelight casts enchanting shadows and a veil of romance over the scene. The table, elegantly set with fine china, crystal glassware, and silverware, beckons me to indulge.

Wowza. Sean really outdid himself.

On the table sits a small blue box with a white bow. It sure looks like a jewelry box. My heart skips a beat at the sight of it.

Is my engagement ring in that box? The thought of it gives me a thrill, and an image of Sean and I making love as I wear nothing but the ring flashes through my mind. Wouldn't that be something? Another thought enters my mind as well. This time, it's a vision of us in the future, both old and gray. We're holding hands as we rock in chairs on a porch, our wedding rings still sparking as a symbol of our love and commitment.

Am I going to say yes?

I am. Yes. I do. I am. I will.

The man who led me back here gestures for me to have a seat, then disappears.

Sean has yet to arrive, and the weight of the jewelry box resting before me fills me with all sorts of emotions. It feels like forever that I wait for him.

Finally, he arrives.

"Miss me, my Darling?" he says as he approaches me from behind and kisses my neck seductively.

"Always," I reply, melting into him.

He's dressed in tight jeans—yum—and a black button-down-shirt with cowboy boots and a hat. He looks the part of a country music star, that's for sure. I'm so happy to see his career dreams coming true. I hope tonight is a special one for him. Buck Davenport must see something special, or else he wouldn't be letting Sean open the show.

"Special night, huh?" I ask as he takes a seat across from me.

"More special than you know," he says with a grin.

I can't help but feel like we're on some kind of reality show, which reminds me. Sean was supposed to be filming me for the docu-series. I don't think he's done a bit of filming since we've been here. I guess you could say we've been preoccupied. I hope Sonny isn't mad.

Sean reaches out and takes my hand, and my arm comes to rest against the blue jewelry box. He sees me notice, so he nods and winks.

"Open it up," he says.

"For me?" I ask coyly. "I didn't want to presume."

Our banter dances like a playful breeze, teasing and enticing. Sean's eyes twinkle mischievously, and a knowing smile curves his lips. The air is alive with anticipation, and I find myself hanging onto his every word, captivated by his charm.

With a flicker of excitement in his eyes, Sean gently taps the jewelry box. "Darling, my love, the moment has arrived. Open it, and let its beauty illuminate our path."

I hold my breath, my heart racing as I slowly lift the lid of the box. The soft candlelight dances upon the dazzling diamonds nestled within. Their brilliance shimmers, casting a mesmerizing glow that mirrors the intensity of our connection.

A gasp escapes my lips as I take in their radiant beauty, my eyes locking with Sean's. He reaches across the table, his fingertips brushing against my hand as he delicately takes the earrings from the box.

"These diamonds symbolize more than just adornment, Clara," Sean says, his voice filled with sincerity. "These earrings are a reflection of your inner light, your strength, and the way you illuminate my world."

A warm flush spreads across my cheeks, and I can't help but feel overwhelmed by the depth of his words. The scenery around us seems to fade away, leaving only the flickering candles, the rhythmic sound of the waves, and the unspoken promises hanging in the air.

With a gentle touch, Sean guides me to stand, his eyes locked with mine. The music of the night surrounds us, the melody of love drawing us closer. I can feel the anticipation building, like a symphony crescendoing towards a breathtaking finale.

"Clara," Sean whispers, his voice filled with tenderness. "May I have this dance? Let's create a memory that will forever be etched in our hearts."

I smile as I place my hand in his, feeling the warmth of his touch. Together, we sway to an invisible rhythm, our bodies moving in synchrony as the world fades away.

In this moment, with the moon casting its gentle glow upon us, I realize that love's grandeur is not found in extravagant gestures or elaborate plans. It resides in the simple, profound moments that weave the fabric of our journey.

"I thought something else might have been in that box," I say softly.

"Did you?" he asks simply, then kisses me passionately. "What would you have said, if something different had been in that box?"

"I would have said yes," I reply.

He exhales sharply, as if my answer means everything to him.

It's interesting, though, because I'm not disappointed, exactly. I don't want things to move too fast. I don't think there's an expiration date on what Sean and I have. In fact, I'm relieved that I will get some more breathing room before we officially become engaged. More time to make plans and adjust to the fact that I'm not part of a duo. Life will be different from now on. I figure it's good to take our time.

For now, we'll remain fake engaged. But that's all.

As we dance beneath the starlit sky, surrounded by the flickering candles and the soft murmur of the ocean, I am grateful for the gift of this night, the beauty of Sean's love, and the shared connection that surpasses any expectations.

We hold each other tightly as we sway.

In this embrace, our hearts beat as one, our souls entwined in a dance of love and possibilities. The radiant glow of the diamond earrings mirrors the sparkle in our eyes, a testament to the magic that blossoms when two souls find their way to each other.

I'm happy. We're happy. *Together.*

I don't care how sappy I sound.

As the night continues to unfold, we dance beneath the moonlit sky, celebrating the connection we share, and savoring every moment of this enchanting love story.

We eat a delicious meal of fresh seafood, then Sean sends me with the same young man who led me to dinner. It's time for Sean Irish to make his debut on stage, and I can't wait to watch it all unfold firsthand.

"New earrings?" Rosie asks as I take my seat in the amphitheater between her and Ella. My parents are seated on the other side Patrick, further down the row. They smile and wave.

I tilt my head so that everyone can see the diamonds sparkle. "From you know who," I say with a huge smile. "You like them?"

"They're gorgeous," Rosie replies. "I just thought—"

"I did, too," I reply. "But I guess we jumped the gun."

Ella chuckles, then pats me on the back gently. "Clarebear, you are lovably naive."

"What makes you say that?"

She clears her throat and lowers her eyes. "Sean didn't fly us and your parents down here just to give you a pair of earrings. You'll see."

CHAPTER 23

SEAN

I find a quiet spot on a wooden bench backstage and collapse onto it. I'm a nervous wreck. Perspiration lines my brow, my heart is pounding, and my mouth is dry like cotton. I hope I can actually sing when it's time to go out there.

If I can get out of my head long enough, I'd notice that the atmosphere around me crackles with excitement. The scent of saltwater permeates the open air, intermingling with the aroma of freshly mown grass. The stage, adorned with vibrant lights, casts a warm, golden glow that illuminates the night sky. The amphitheater, nestled on the pristine shores of Seven Mile Beach, provides a breathtaking backdrop for this monumental moment.

My heart beats with a mixture of anticipation and nervous energy. This is the night I've been working towards, my first performance as Sean Irish. I'm ready to make my mark on the world of country music.

Luckily or unluckily, depending on how you look at

it, I don't have much time to ruminate. A member of the stage crew grabs me and practically throws a guitar into my hands. Before I can protest or ask for more time, I'm being pushed onto the stage.

Dear God, please let this go well. Please keep me from embarrassing myself—and Clara—spectacularly.

"You're on," the stagehand says as she shoves me forward.

"Okay," I mumble, working to find my confidence and my voice.

As I step into the spotlight, the energy of the crowd washes over me, heightening my senses.

Buck Davenport is on stage to introduce me. "Ladies and gentleman," he says, "You know many of the songs this man has written, but you haven't seen his face or heard his voice until now. Tonight, I'm proud to introduce you to the talented Mr. Sean Irish!"

He stretches out my name, making it sound dramatic and fancy. I must admit, it has a nice ring to it. Clara hit the nail on the head when she came up with it.

That's my girl.

I raise a hand to shield my eyes from the bright lights. I find Clara out there, in the row of seats I reserved for her and her people. *Our people.* I nod and wave. When I do, squeals of delight erupt from people around them.

I guess I have a lot to get used to when it comes to being on stage as an artist instead of behind the scenes as a songwriter.

All in good time.

The first notes of my guitar reverberate through the

air, blending seamlessly with the rhythmic crashing of waves. The crowd, a sea of eager faces, erupts in a thunderous applause. Their energy fuels me, and I channel it into every strum of the guitar, every lyric that escapes my lips.

The melodies I play resonate with the spirit of the island. The twang of the guitar strings carries the soulful essence of country music, intertwining with the cool ocean breeze. The music becomes a living, breathing entity, wrapping itself around the hearts of the audience, capturing their emotions and transporting them to a place where love and music collide.

It feels incredible to be the conduit making the connections.

As the performance of my set reaches its crescendo, I feel a surge of confidence and determination. The song I wrote for Clara, a heartfelt declaration of our love, is next. I take the mic in hand to introduce the song … and my Darling.

"This next song was written for a special someone in my life," I say. "She's here tonight, and I want y'all to meet her. Clara Darling, will you join me on stage, please?"

A spotlight finds Clara, who looks excited as she climbs over her friends and into the aisle. An usher helps clear the path as she makes her way to me. When she reaches the stage, I scoop her into my arms and kiss her deeply.

"Nice earrings," I whisper.

She smiles.

I look around, suddenly realizing that she'll be left

standing here a long time while I sing. "Can we get her a stool?" I ask.

"Great minds think alike," Buck says as he brings a stool out to the middle of the stage and helps Clara climb onto it.

Clara is a bit starstruck to be so close to Buck Davenport, but she thanks him politely and returns her attention to me.

"Good luck, buddy," Buck says as he gives me fist bump then disappears backstage.

I close my eyes and take a deep breath, to center myself. Clara and the crowd is hanging on my every word. They're eagerly waiting for whatever will happen next. Mobile phones glow brightly as many people in the audience hold theirs in the air to record. Maybe we can share some of the footage with Sonny.

"Do it!" someone shouts, causing the crowd to erupt into nervous laughter.

"Okay, okay," I say. "Go easy on me, y'all. It isn't every day I ask the love of my life to marry me."

With that, Clara's eyes go so wide I think they might pop right out of her head.

"But first, I'm gonna sing her the song I wrote. Here goes."

I strum the beginning chords of my guitar. I wanted the first few minutes to be acoustic, so the band waits patiently behind me for their cue.

I sing slowly, with all of my heart.

In a world that's uncertain, where shadows may creep,

Our love is a fortress, a bond we will keep.
Give me your doubts, I'll silence every fear,
Together we'll conquer, side by side, my dear.

Give me your worst, I'll give you my best,
Let me get to you first, you can forget all the rest.
United we'll stand, we won't divide and won't fall,
Be my darling, my love, let's climb right over these walls.

In the face of the storms, we'll find our own peace,
Our hearts intertwined, never seeking release.
Through highs and through lows, we'll weather the test,
Our love's a refuge, a place we find rest.

WITH EACH STRUM and every heartfelt lyric, the connection between the audience and me grows stronger. Their voices rise in unison, singing along to the chorus that has become a part of their collective story. The energy pulsates through the open-air amphitheater, transforming it into a haven of pure magic.

I continue to sing.

Give me your worst, I'll give you my best,
Let me get to you first, you can forget all the rest.
United we'll stand, we won't divide and won't fall,
Be my darling, my love, let's climb right over these walls.

Hand in hand, we'll face the unknown,
Our love, a shelter that's uniquely our own.
With you by my side, we'll conquer all strife,

Together, we'll create a beautiful life.

Give me your worst, I'll give you my best,
Let me get to you first, you can forget all the rest.
United we'll stand, we won't divide and won't fall,
Be my darling, my love, let's climb right over these walls.

AS THE SONG CONCLUDES, the crowd erupts in thunderous applause, their hearts touched by the raw emotion and authenticity of the lyrics. The melody lingers in the air, its powerful message of unity and love resonating deep within their souls.

In that moment, I realize that the journey of our love is just beginning. Together, Clara and I will navigate life's twists and turns. As the final notes of the song fade away, I know that our love story, like the music we create, will continue to unfold in beautiful and unexpected ways.

And then, the moment arrives. The final chorus approaches, and I know it's time to unveil the surprise that will forever change our lives. With a surge of adrenaline, I step away from the microphone. Time seems to stand still as I drop to one knee, the atmosphere thick with emotion and hope.

"My Darling, my love, will you marry me?" I ask, my voice filled with sincerity, the words resonating with every fiber of my being.

A collective gasp ripples through the crowd, their breaths held in anticipation. Clara's eyes well with tears, a radiant smile illuminating her face. She extends her hand, her touch a lifeline that connects us in this pivotal moment.

I open another small blue jewelry box, this one containing a diamond engagement ring. I carefully take it out and slide it onto Clara's finger.

Her response, a resounding yes, fills the air, carried by a chorus of cheers and applause. The amphitheater comes alive with collective joy.

In that magical moment, under the starlit sky, surrounded by the energy of the crowd and the music that binds us, we embrace. The cheers and applause reverberate through the amphitheater, echoing the celebration of our love.

Tears of joy fill my eyes and wet my cheeks. There's more to my surprise, and I had better get on with it.

I rise to the mic again. "Hold on, y'all. This ain't all. Like my Uncle Finn always says, go big or go home, right?"

The crowd cheers me on.

"Here goes nothing," I say as I motion to members of the stage crew in the back who are waiting on my cue.

They jump into action. Crew members dressed in all black appear with a wedding dress and tuxedo in hand as a makeshift altar appears from the back of the stage.

Upon seeing this, the crowd cheers enthusiastically. They start chanting the word wedding over and over again.

Wedding. Wedding. Wedding.

I look at Clara, searching her eyes for a reaction. But she looks stunned, like a deer in headlights.

I lift the mic. "My Darling, if you'll have me, I'd like to marry you right here and now. On this stage. With Buck Davenport officiating. He's ordained, thanks to the internet."

The crowd goes absolutely wild. Clara remains silent.

Oh, no.

She begins to shake her head as she slowly backs away.

"Darling?" I ask, taking a few steps to follow her. I'm all wired up for the mics and can't go far.

She turns toward the stairs, and I'm not sure what she's thinking.

"I can't do this," she says, and she runs off the stage and out of the amphitheater with a speed I didn't know she was capable of.

The crowd goes silent as I stand alone. My heart is broken.

I pushed too hard. Too far.

What have I done?

CLARA

Grand Cayman Island
Day 7

Two Days Later

I sit alone in our suite, the silence enveloping me like a heavy blanket. My heart aches with the weight of what feels like a terrible loss. In my mind, I play out a vivid scenario, a glimpse into a future without Sean by my side.

I imagine seeing him on the film crew back home in Loveland at The Romantics building, his infectious laughter and mischievous charm captivating those around him. The image is bittersweet, as I realize I'll no longer be the one to share those moments, to be the recipient of his playful banter and affectionate glances.

As I watch him from a distance in my imagination, a

pang of sadness washes over me. The easy camaraderie he shares with the crew reminds me of the connection we once had, and it hurts to think that it may be lost forever.

I imagine the mornings, waking up to an empty space beside me. The absence of his warmth and his touch leaving an indelible void. The thought of navigating life without his steadying presence brings a profound sense of loneliness.

In this imagined future, I see myself trying to move on, attempting to fill the void with distractions and superficial connections. But the emptiness lingers, a constant reminder of what once was and what could have been.

I see myself attending events, my eyes scanning the room for a glimpse of him, only to find disappointment in his absence. The realization that he's moved on, that our paths have diverged, cuts deep, and tears threaten to spill from my eyes.

I imagine hearing stories about his adventures, his successes, and his new love. Each mention of his name feels like a dagger to my heart, a reminder of what I've lost. The pain intensifies, fueling a longing that cannot be quelled.

Hours later, I'm still curled in the bed Sean and I once shared as Rosie attempts to comfort me. She's talking to him on the phone so I don't have to.

"Tell him I've packed his things," I say. "I'll leave his bags with the staff at the front desk."

The morning light filters through the curtains, casting a soft glow in the room. I sit on the edge of the bed, my heart heavy with the weight of my decision. Rosie holds the phone to her ear, her eyes filled with concern as she listens to Sean's voice on the other end of the line.

"He says he's sorry, Clara," Rosie relays, her voice gentle. "He wants to talk to you, to explain."

I shake my head, my gaze fixed on the floor. "I can't, Rosie. Not right now. It's all too much, too fast."

Rosie nods understandingly, knowing the turmoil that's been churning within me. She places the phone on the nightstand, her hand resting on mine in a comforting gesture.

"He loves you, Clara. I've seen it in his eyes, in the way he's cared for you. Give yourself some time to process everything, but remember, love is worth fighting for."

Tears well in my eyes, and I look at Rosie, grateful for her unwavering support. "I know," I whisper, my voice barely audible. "But I need to find my own path, to understand what I truly want."

Just then, Ella enters the room, her presence a ray of light amidst the shadows. She embraces me tightly, her warmth enveloping me like a protective shield.

"We're here for you, Clara," Ella says, her voice filled with sincerity. "Whatever you decide, we'll support you wholeheartedly. Even your bitchy mom supports you. She and your dad are out playing tennis right now, but they said to call if you need anything at all."

That makes me laugh. "Tennis? They really are stepping out of their comfort zone."

I take a deep breath, feeling the weight of their love

and understanding surrounding me. In this moment of uncertainty, I find solace in the presence of my friends.

I'm glad Sean brought them down here. I just wish he hadn't pulled that stunt with the wedding on stage. That was way too much. It freaked me out.

After a few moments, Rosie's phone buzzes with a text notification. She picks it up and her eyes widen in surprise. "It's from Sean."

My heart skips a beat, curiosity mingling with trepidation. "What does he say?"

Rosie's lips curl into a smile as she reads aloud, "Tell Clara I'm on my way to the airport and will be out of here shortly. But if she will, ask her to meet there in an hour, at the spot where we stepped off the plane and out into this tropical paradise together. Let's talk. No pressure, just two people trying to figure things out. I have something to give her. I was going to give it to her after the concert, but well, we all know how that turned out."

I glance at the nightstand where the engagement ring Sean gave me sits in its tiny blue box. Hope flickers within me. "What could he possibly want to give me?"

Ella shrugs, then grabs Rosie's phone and pushes the button to call Sean. "Only one way to find out."

"What are you doing?" I ask.

"Hush," she says, waving me off.

I fold my arms over my chest and fume. I'm also curious. What could it be?

"Hey Sean," Ella says when he answers. "You're on speaker. What is it that you want to give to Clara?"

He clears his throat. Now he knows that I'm listening. Things feel strangely intimate, yet also not.

"It's something she's wanted, so I got it for her. Like I said in my text, I was going to give it to her after the concert. I'm on my way to Fort Myers, Florida now, though, and can't really take it with me."

We hear a lot of background noise, and then the unmistakable sound of a little woof.

I jump up. "Caroline?" I ask, instantly knowing I'm right.

"That's her," Sean replies. "I know I shouldn't have, but I already did. I can't abandon the poor girl."

Rosie narrows her eyes, working to catch up. "Caroline is a puppy?"

I nod.

"Okay, bye bye," Sean says. "Hope to see you in an hour, my Darling."

He hangs up the phone. I suppose he's tired of waiting on me. I suppose I don't blame him.

Ella tosses the phone down on the bed and shakes her head. "This doesn't add up," she says. "I meant what I said about supporting you no matter what, but frankly, Clara, I think you're being a twat."

"Ella!" Rosie shouts. "Easy."

Ella shrugs. "I don't think she needs it easy right now. I think a little tough love is in order."

She reaches for Rosie's phone again and I think she's going to call Sean back, but instead, she calls Sonny. He answers right away.

"Rosalie?" he asks.

"It's Ella, but Rosie is here, too," Ella says.

"What can I do for you ladies?" Sonny asks cheerfully. "I hope you're all enjoying island life."

"We are," Ella replies, her no-nonsense persona in full force. "Quick question. Did you send Sean O'Shea on assignment in Fort Myers, Florida?"

It's presumptuous to call Sonny and ask a question like that. Where he send Sean on assignment isn't actually any of our business. He doesn't seem to mind, though, and he answers.

"No, I didn't. But his Uncle Finn lives in nearby Sanibel Island and I hear they're going to take him off of life support. He was in a bad motorcycle accident last week. Sean talked about his uncle in the car when I drove him to the airport, but didn't mention the accident until we talked on the phone yesterday. Apparently, Uncle Finn never married or had kids even though he'd always wanted to. I think the whole thing has Sean spooked."

"Great, thank you so much, Sonny," Ella says. "See you at home in a few days."

Sonny barely has time to say goodbye before she ends the call.

"There you have it," Ella says matter of factly. "The guy moved too fast because his uncle is dying. Is that really such an unforgivable offense, Clara? I think you should cut him some slack."

My eyes grow wider than they did at the concert when that alter appeared. "Wow," I mumble. "I had no idea. He was trying to show me pictures of his family and I sort of brushed him off. Now I feel terrible. I didn't realize Uncle Finn was hurt. I wish I could do that over."

Rosie smiles at me sweetly. "It isn't too late to make things right."

I sigh and bury my face into a pillow. "But I made a fool of him. Of us," I say.

"Do you love him?" Rosie asks.

"Yes, very much."

"Do you want to spend the rest of your life with him?"

"I do," I say. "I said yes on stage, remember? Even though all of that was way, way, way out of my comfort zone. Have you met me? I'm Clara, the shy girl who likes to play it safe."

Ella reaches over and slaps my ass, hard. "Not anymore," she says. "Get yourself showered and dressed in something pretty. We're going to the airport to get your man."

"And Caroline," I say with a smile.

"And Caroline," Rosie echos. "I hope she'll get along well with Penny."

Ella laughs and shakes her head. "The Romantics have gone to the dogs."

At that, we all laugh.

"Maybe we're growing up," I say. "Took us long enough."

Rosie glances at Ella playfully. "You know what this means, right?"

"I know!" raising my hand like a schoolkid. "It means you're next, Ella."

She swats at us as we all laugh together.

I excuse myself to shower and dress. When I return,

my friends have all of my things packed and piled by the door.

"What's this?" I ask.

"Keep up, Clara," Ella says. "You're going to Sanibel Island with your fiance. We packed you a small bag. We'll take the rest of your things home with us. That is, after I find some local man candy and enjoy a good romp on the beach. I'm sure Rosie and Patrick can keep each other busy while I play."

What would I do without my two best friends? No matter what life brings, we face it together.

I love them. And I love Sean. And Caroline. I can't wait to see her sweet little face.

I take a deep breath, gathering my courage. "Okay," I say, a sense of resolve infusing my voice. "Let's go."

CHAPTER 25

CLARA

As we reach the spot where Sean and I first stepped out into the island sunshine, I see him standing there, his gaze fixed on the horizon. In his arms is the cutest gray and white ball of fluff I've ever seen.

Caroline. Our baby.

I approach slowly, my heart pounding with a mixture of uncertainty and hope. Sean turns towards me, his eyes filled with a vulnerability I've never seen before.

"Clara," he says, his voice soft, laced with a tinge of regret. "I want you to know that I never meant to overwhelm you. I love you, and I'm willing to take whatever time you need."

I study his face, searching for sincerity, for the depth of his feelings. In that moment, the walls around my heart start to crumble, and I realize that despite the doubts and fears, love still exists between us.

He thinks he's the one who messed things up, but I blame myself. This man has done everything in his power to make me happy and give me everything I want in life. And I rejected him in front of thousands of people.

I feel terrible.

"Sean," I respond, my voice filled with a mixture of emotion and determination. "I need time to sort through my feelings, to understand what I want. But I know for a fact that includes you. It includes us. If you'll still have me. I didn't know about your Uncle Finn until Sonny told Ella a little while ago. I'm so sorry."

He chokes up, unable to speak. I shift my attention to the wriggling puppy in his arms.

"Caroline?" I breathe, my voice filled with disbelief and joy.

Sean nods, his eyes shining with excitement. "I wanted to surprise you, my Darling. Meet your new companion."

"Our new companion," I say.

He nods, then wipes a tear from his eyes.

I reach out, my hands trembling with anticipation, and Sean gently places the adorable sheepadoodle puppy in my arms. Caroline nuzzles against me, her soft fur and warm breath reminding me that love can come in many forms.

A crowd has formed around us and erupts in cheers and applause. I feel a rush of emotion as I see that Rosie, Patrick, Ella, and my parents are all there, front and center. The weight of my imagined future without Sean dissipates, replaced by a renewed sense of hope and determination.

I take a deep breath, and with Caroline nestled in my arms, I look into Sean's eyes. The melody of the song he wrote for me echoes in my mind, and I know that this is the perfect moment to show him how deeply I still feel.

Clearing my throat, I steady my voice and begin to sing. The lyrics flow effortlessly, the words carrying the depth of my emotions:

In a world that's spinning, where time rushes by,
We'll slow down the moments, never questioning why.
Give me your dreams, I'll make them take flight,
Our love, a symphony, playing through the night.

Give me your worst, I'll give you my best,
Let me get to you first, you can forget all the rest.
United we'll stand, we won't divide and won't fall,
Be my darling, my love, let's climb right over these walls.

Through the highs and lows, we'll dance with grace,
Every step, a testament, our love's embrace.
Give me your doubts, let them dissipate,
In our hearts, forever, love will resonate.

Give me your worst, I'll give you my best,
Let me get to you first, you can forget all the rest.
United we'll stand, we won't divide and won't fall,
Be my darling, my love, let's climb right over these walls.

In a world of uncertainties, love will prevail,
Our bond unbreakable, it will never fail.
Through the years that unfold, we'll navigate,
With love as our compass, we'll never deviate.

Give me your worst, I'll give you my best,
Let me get to you first, you can forget all the rest.
United we'll stand, we won't divide and won't fall,
Be my darling, my love, let's climb right over these walls.

With each passing day, our love will grow,
A melody of passion, forever to show.
Together, we'll write our love's symphony,
Our hearts entwined, forever you and me.

As the last notes of the verse hang in the air, Sean's eyes widen with surprise and delight. He joins in, our voices blending in harmony as we sing the chorus together, united in our love.

"You sing beautifully, my Darling," he says through tears. "We should sing together sometime. We could be Irish Darlings or The Darling Irish. Or something. I don't care, as long as we're together."

The crowd's cheers grow louder, the waves of support and love washing over us. And in that moment, surrounded by our friends and family, I realize that this is where I truly belong— in Sean's arms, with Caroline by our side.

With tears of joy streaming down my cheeks, I close the distance between us and wrap my arms around

Sean. The embrace feels like a homecoming, a reassurance that our love has weathered the storm and emerged stronger than ever.

"Just give me a little time before the wedding. Okay?"

He nods, kissing me. His lips feel so good on mine.

I take the ring box out of my pocket and hand it to him.

"Ask me again," I say.

He does just that, dropping to one knee and asking for my hand in marriage as little Caroline woofs her approval.

The moment stretches, time standing still as we bask in the overwhelming sense of love and connection. And as the crowd continues to cheer, our loved ones gathering around us, I know that we have created a moment that will forever be etched in our hearts.

Together, we step into a future filled with endless possibilities, supported by the love of those who believe in us. Caroline wriggles happily in my arms, a symbol of the joy and adventure that awaits us.

With the sounds of laughter and celebration surrounding us, we know that our love story is far from over. We have learned that even in the face of uncertainty, love has the power to overcome, to create a symphony of joy, and to bring us back to where we belong—in each other's arms.

Hand in hand, hearts entwined, we walk forward, ready to embrace the journey that lies ahead. And as we continue on this path of love, we know that together, we can conquer anything, creating a melody of love that will resonate throughout our lives.

"Where are we going?" Sean asks as we step into the airport.

"Sanibel Island to join your family, of course," I say. "Just as soon as I figure out how to take this baby dog with me. Can she ride under the seat?"

We turn and wave to our loved ones who have gathered on the island to support us, then we walk into the airport for the next of what will turn out to be many plane rides together.

The following summer, we will return to Grand Cayman Island with even more friends and family … to get married.

THE END.

* * *

Get the next book in the series at
BrightHappyLove.com:

Yes Rehearsal

The Romantics, Book 3

Happy reading!

ABOUT THE AUTHOR

Blissfully in love with her real life Prince Charming for a quarter century and counting, Kelly Bright knows a thing or two about happily ever after.

She believes love conquers all and that there's someone special out there for every single one of us. She writes emotional, feel good romantic comedy.

When her head isn't buried in a romantic book or movie, you'll likely find Kelly with Mr. Bright—scoping out charming settings for her next story or chatting up other meant-to-be couples and learning how they met.

Connect with Kelly at BrightHappyLove.com, and

on Instagram, Facebook, and TikTok at @brighthappylove.